PENGUIN BOOKS
BOO

Shinie Antony has authored the short-story collections *The Orphanage for Words, Barefoot and Pregnant* and the novels *When Mira Went Forth and Multiplied* and *A Kingdom for His Love*. She has compiled the anthology *Why We Don't Talk*. Co-founder of the Bangalore Literature Festival and director of the Bengaluru Poetry Festival, she won the Commonwealth Short Story Asia region prize in 2003 for her story 'A Dog's Death'. Her novel *The Girl Who Couldn't Love* will be out this year.

13 STORIES THAT WILL
SEND A CHILL DOWN YOUR SPINE

EDITED BY SHINIE ANTONY

PENGUIN BOOKS

An imprint of Penguin Random House

PENGUIN BOOKS

USA | Canada | UK | Ireland | Australia
New Zealand | India | South Africa | China | Singapore

Penguin Books is part of the Penguin Random House group of companies
whose addresses can be found at global.penguinrandomhouse.com

Published by Penguin Random House India Pvt. Ltd
4th Floor, Capital Tower 1, MG Road,
Gurugram 122 002, Haryana, India

Penguin
Random House
India

First published in Penguin Books by Penguin Random House India 2017

ISBN 9780143441717

Typeset in Adobe Jenson Pro by Manipal Digital Systems, Manipall

Printed at Manipal Technologies Limited, India

www.penguin.co.in

MIX
Paper | Supporting
responsible forestry
FSC® C043100

This is a legitimate digitally printed version of the book and therefore might not
have certain extra finishing on the cover.

For the invisible fingers that brush against ours

Contents

CONTENTS

Introduction

The unknown has always beckoned. Infinite, cobwebby, black as the night, silent as the grave, what we cannot see hear touch. What, furthermore, is perhaps not alive.

My own experiences of the uncanny stay mine; fear takes me where it will. There were whispers without words and things I almost saw. And unlike what I always thought, squeamish as I am and lily-livered, these semi-happenings did not creep me out. Sometimes I saw them as other-worldly warnings, sometimes they were not meant to be seen and my eye had somehow breached a divide, sometimes my mouth formed words I did not mean to say . . .

The paranormal has many subgenres, but of these it was not the occult, poltergeists or screams of the possessed that brought me to these stories, but the psychological thrill. The mind is where it all begins. The mind is where it lives. This feeling that there's something out there—and it is on to us. It knows that we know. And we must forever pretend we don't know, not catch its eye—even when it is looking straight at us.

INTRODUCTION

The gothic charm of K.R. Meera's story, the sweet smell of onions in Kanishk Tharoor's tale, the burden of hindsight in Shashi Deshpande's mythofiction, the menacing narrator in Jerry Pinto's story—they all bring in the supernatural slyly, stylishly. Durjoy Datta, Jahnavi Barua, Manabendra Bandyopadhyay, Kiran Manral and Jaishree Misra give us the old-fashioned traditional ghost story, the one where the banshee sighs or screams. While Ipsita Roy Chakraverti decodes a message from the beyond, Madhavi S. Mahadevan and Usha K.R. take us to places where the backstory is everything.

We wouldn't be here—you reading this, me writing this—if we didn't know. Despite science, reason and a raised eyebrow. Deep in our bones, when all falls silent, there is a knowing that precedes births and lingers after deaths. It lifts the hair at the nape of our neck; it stares at us, infatuated, from behind stairs; prescient, it invades our very rocking chair, replacing peace and calm with a restless zigzag; it rotates its head 360 degrees when we aren't looking.

It doesn't dispel though we move on, go our ways, live lives, love and let go. What is it that shifts just beyond our vision? Who listens when we talk in our heads? When does dark get just that little bit darker? Why that word on the billboard—the same word we just finished thinking about? And then bumping into the very person we thought of after a hundred years only that morning . . .

What do we know about ourselves besides incidents and milestones and birthdays and heartbreaks, what do we know of that which cannot be known?

It is there in a photograph or painting you see—the feeling that you've been there before, seen that face somewhere. We are here but we are elsewhere too.

A haunting. Begins as a catch in the side, a stiff neck, a hunch, a bad feeling, pins and needles, an eye twitch, sleep talk, a leg gone numb, vertigo, spasms, heart that trebles its beat, a smell, a chill, a spell, a tingle, dreaming the same dream, a sudden vision of what's to come, waking at 3.33 a.m., a song no one else can hear, the sound of breathing when we hold our breath . . .

We are never alone, are we?

HE-GHOUL

K.R. Meera

K.R. Meera has published five collections of short stories, two novellas, five novels and two children's books. She won the Kerala Sahitya Akademi Award (2009) for her short story 'Ave Maria'. Her novel *Aarachaar* received several awards, including the Kerala Sahitya Akademi Award (2013), Odakkuzhal Award (2013), Vayalar Award (2014) and Kendra Sahitya Akademi Award (2015). Its translation *Hangwoman* was shortlisted for the DSC Prize for South Asian Literature (2016). Her latest novella, *The Poison of Love*, is longlisted for the 2017 DSC Prize for South Asian Literature.

She set out for the bungalow where her first lover was killed. She went alone. Some journeys, of course, *must* be solitary.

The day had already perished when they turned from the main road towards the estate where the anthills crept out from the depths of the earth. She saw it from afar—the bungalow that crouched in the dark like a bestial creature with yellow-tinged eyes at the very end of the dirt road that twisted and turned like the swirling interior of a labyrinth. Trees and thickets on both sides of the road stood still, petrified, covered with sticky black clotted blood that seeped from twilight's severed neck. She heard something leap inside the wilderness once, and then again. Suddenly, a grotesque bird with a bloated head flashed right across the road with what sounded like a cry of rage. A dog barked frantically somewhere.

The caretaker, appointed by the new owner of the bungalow, and his wife were waiting for her under the tall arches of the portico. They saw that she was alone. Instantly terrified, they tried to persuade her to return in the same taxi. This was the scene of a horrific murder; nobody stays here by themselves; three people who once stayed here overnight are dead—they tried to scare her. It didn't touch her. Anyway, after that first relationship had ended, it was as if she was entombed in a glass coffin. People saw her. She saw them. But no one, nothing, could touch her. She struggled constantly for breath inside the coffin. She had sought out the bungalow precisely to shatter it. Therefore, she chose to spend the night in the bedroom her lover had slept in that fateful night.

She put on the lingerie she had chosen, many years ago, for that last rendezvous. The steps leading down to the cellar were next to the staircase, which climbed up from the drawing room with its tall marble pillars and arches, wound in a semicircle around the entire dining room and ended near the kitchen. After dinner, when she stood gazing at the antelope heads on the drawing room walls, the caretaker's wife came up to her to mark her forehead with kumkum from the Mariamman temple and tie a piece of blessed string around her wrist. That made her flinch. Her lover had also anointed her forehead with kumkum before their first lovemaking. Once the caretaker and his wife went out to the watcher's shed, she was all alone. She untied the string from her wrist, wiped off the kumkum. Then she strained to imagine into presence her lover's lost soul. Sex and fear were the same to her. She could not feel either until they were roused to fullness in and through her imagination.

But the ghoul revealed himself only after she had fallen asleep. A dog howled and woke her up. A thousand dogs howled after that, one by one. It was pitch-dark all around. A scream flew up from below the stairs. Then, a scary silence crept everywhere. She got up and opened the door to the balcony. The French windows stood completely open, and also the door to the corridor. Someone was running, panting.

Then, at the very end of the corridor, he appeared. She started, and snapped, 'Who's that?'

He vanished. She went back into her room and shut the door, suspecting a thief, and picked up her mobile phone, scanning it for signs of a signal. Her mind focused on what to do if the thief broke in; her heart thundered. It had pounded thus only at their last rendezvous, she remembered. Don't thunder like this at the presence of a mere thief, she scolded her heart. The wind blew harshly. As if infuriated by her indifference, it pulled down the objects on her table, pulled free her tied-up tresses, tugged up her nightdress, and made her gasp for breath as it forced dust into her eyes and nose. Instantly, she realized that it was her lover-turned-ghoul that she had run into. Opening the door, she stepped into the balcony and, from there, turned into the corridor. Suddenly, the lights blacked out. Darkness invaded every corner. She kept moving forward. She imagined her lover-ghoul sucking her lifeblood, killing her. That would be such a romantic way to die. She too would embrace death in the very same bungalow where he was killed. Her blood would spread over the scars of his dried-up blood on the floor. Maybe no one will believe this; maybe he didn't deserve it at all—but what a tale of love, so intense!

That house of glass windows and crystal cupboards was built way back, when kings still ruled. Just a few months ago, the relative of a friend had bought it for a song. The rooms were filled with the musty odour of termites. She had noticed a large candle and a matchbox on the dining table at dinner. So she went towards the dining table in the dark, found the matchbox, and lit a matchstick. For the first time in her life, she saw a He-Ghoul. A man of glass, a hollow man. Of no flesh, no marrow, no hair on its head, no fangs, no blood-dripping tongue. A body fissured and fragmented. A neck that looked as if it would snap at any moment. Whitish and motionless eyeballs deep in their sockets. Anyone else would have screamed in fright seeing him. She felt no fear. What was terrifying was the sheer hardness of the He-Ghoul's face, its very hollowness and its naked inferiority, impossible to hide even after death. Even when he's a ghoul, a man is a man; he shows off more than what he's got.

He was playing He-Man before her now, stretching his body tall, beyond the bungalow's upper storey. He raised his brittle arms of glass above the darkened ceiling. As vain as ever, he held his crumbling neck erect. 'Admit it! I am the stronger one even now!'—that was a silent plea, but it resounded everywhere. In a final gesture of frustration, he pulled off a ceiling fan and flung it down. It nearly hit her, but he knocked it aside and went all billowy, as though he had done her a great favour. For this favour, should you not forget the crimes I committed when I was alive? he asked her soundlessly. Should you not be grateful? That amused her. She had loved him so when he was alive; she had been ready to die for him, deluded that he deserved the highest sacrifice. Now she imagined courting death for this lover long dead. What a poetic death that would be. Embracing the end in the very same cellar in which he died just before he was to step on to a high pedestal in politics! She would seize him from the blazing depths of hell. Even if that were impossible, even if that would make her scorn herself, what a love story it would be, one that could mesmerize the masses! The He-Ghoul vanished suddenly. Maybe he was convinced now that he could no longer awaken her love. The wind blew again, hard. The flame of the candle died, and the pitch-black and the quiet rolled right back. The sounds of something falling on the floor here and there rang in the room. Outside, the muffled screams of a thousand gasping children. From the rooms above, terrifying sounds. She watched with bated breath. It was clear that he was trying to scare her. A ghoul maybe, but a man can only be a man. He tries to scare, attack those whose love he cannot command. And whether or not he secures their love, he makes them bow to him.

Something struck her on the head and she fell on the floor. Heavy objects kept raining from the ceiling. Her ribs were crushed, and in the searing pain, she fainted for a second. Ghoul indeed, she mocked, laughing. At least once, face me directly. Instead of stabbing me in the back. Play the game right, play it fair. Sink your teeth into the same part of the neck that you once kissed. The sounds ceased as if they were blown out. The bungalow fell mute. A man may be a ghoul, but a man can only be a man. He'll strut about, claiming even that some failures are actually victories. She got up, lit the candle again, pulled a chair and sat down at the dining table. In the dim light, the painted pillars of the drawing room cast shadows that twisted menacingly. The crystal windows of the showcases, which bore copper statuettes tinted a bluish green, glinted and reflected the yellow candlelight in all sorts of ways. Then, in the chair opposite, the He-Ghoul appeared bit by bit.

His body of glass shards glowed red, as though fresh from a furnace. On his broken neck, blood smouldered like live coals. She felt sorry for him. This was not how she had expected his He-Ghoul to be. She would have once again liked to see him tall as a tree and bigger than the bungalow. Was a He-Ghoul so puny?

She suppressed a laugh. That provoked him. He began to blaze. Flames leapt from his eyes. His mouth flew open and a huge torch of flame burst out. She didn't bother to be afraid. No man can kill a woman twice. He was a ghoul even when he was alive. But those days he used to be a bunch of very many ghouls, ghouls of others. Now he was just his own ghoul. More cruel than before. But more helpless and weak too. He shook his head and snarled. The coward. Scaring others to cover up the shiver inside.

The flames kept flying out of his mouth. She imagined herself burning in one of them. Surely, a grand, emotional death. Covered in flames, she would embrace him. He too would burn, and to dust they would return—together. Even if that were absurd, even if that was insulting to her, what a heart-shattering saga of love!

For her, his soul had killed itself long before his body was murdered. But before that, he had killed her soul. After that shattering, fragmenting experience of immense pain, the only emotion she had felt was disgust, towards her own self and others. To love and be loved, one needed to love oneself. She felt that she was permanently steeped in a septic tank. The faeces of unknown people covered her from head to foot. On some days, she washed herself again and again and thrust her fingers into her throat, vomiting repeatedly. She found a job abroad, never returned, and spent years avoiding everyone she knew. Until an old friend sought her out and told her of his death, she knew nothing.

She searched the online archives of newspapers and found out about it. It was a pathetic end. The body was recovered three days after his demise from the cellar of the locked bungalow. The head hung pitifully, still joined to the neck, but threatening to separate any minute. There were signs that the killers had tried to chop the body into parts and burn them. It was only when she read that the chest on which she had once reclined, whispering poetry, was free of wounds that she want to throw up again. She threw up and dozed off, tired. When she woke up, she felt that he was standing before her. He was naked. That's how he was etched in her memory. On that full-moon night, in the houseboat he had rented, they had read books leaning on each other, and talked, talked for long. After making love, watching the moonlight fall and the fireflies dance to make a nest in a place where the boat was anchored, he went into the bathroom and came out naked. So she had imagined his He-Ghoul to be naked also. But the He-Ghoul had no organ. So she wasn't sure if he was naked. Maybe He-Ghouls don't need organs to hurt others.

The He-Ghoul grew uneasy, as if he'd read her thoughts. The bungalow began to shake from top to bottom. An angry cry that commanded her to leave rang silently. She laughed in contempt. She imagined herself spending the rest of her life, dying as a wizened old crone, in the bungalow where her lover had been killed. What an electrifying end that would be! Every night, she would rouse him with her memories. He would wander uneasily with a half-severed neck, fire bursting out of his eyes and nose and mouth. Even if it were meaningless, even if it were suicidal of her, what a brilliantly passionate death!

The wind turned even more violent. The trees near the bungalow danced like peacocks and screamed in strange voices. Tomcats dashed in, emitting throat-rending, male-sounding yowls. Their yellow eyes gleamed demonically. They drooled at her, sucking at their blood-red tongues. The He-Ghoul was readying himself for the next attack, she sensed. Ghouls have only the past. Those who are alive have the possibilities of the present, hopes for the future. They have the desire to escape the past. Remembering how this man had always hovered around naked, whenever someone entered her life, made her feel vengeful. Unable to love, to be loved, unable to touch, to be touched, incapable of joy and pride, entombed in a crystal coffin of his shape, how long had she struggled for breath, like a moth trapped in a bottle!

The He-Ghoul became more energetic, as though he had read her mind. Shaking that head so that it was perilously close to falling, he emitted even more fire. The back coverings of the chairs went up in flames. Light filled the room. The tablecloth, the carpet and her nightdress were now ablaze. She moved towards the cellar. Going down the stairs, she turned around and looked at the He-Ghoul. He was confounded, tired. Wanting and not wanting to go down, he thrashed about in pain. She felt stronger. The cellar was filled with the light from the flames that were leaping up her nightdress. It looked like the scene of a very recent murder. The nauseating stink of burnt flesh lingered in there. The cement floor, where he was hacked to death, was wet with blood.

Was this where they laid you down to be chopped up? she asked. The He-Ghoul went round and round the room, spitting fire; he jumped on her. She felt the whiplash of electricity on her skin; she felt the slivers of lightning pierce her flesh. She collapsed. The floor coated with your blood— she rolled on the ground laughing madly. Lying there, she thought of the last night on the houseboat. Like then, she raised her face, looked. She remembered how he'd come out of the bathroom, naked. He'd made love to her, gone out. She remembered how, then, two of his friends from the political field had entered. And how, after two days, she'd opened her eyes in a city hospital. How the police complaint had ended up nowhere, with no evidence. How she was shamed before the world and her family. She felt the flames rise inside her, too.

She thought again of the day he died. He had gone to bed in a room upstairs. Someone had injected him with a sedative. His enemies were hiding in the cellar. He was dragged down there. He struggled awake. They cut his throat in cold blood. Reading her thoughts, the He-Ghoul grew angrier. Giving it one last try, he blew a stream of fire into her eyes. She too flew into a rage. Do you remember your wife coming down to identify your body? she asked. It was almost as if she was determined to let the world know she cared nothing for your death. She did not weep or shudder. She identified your body. Chatted with acquaintances. Barely three months passed before she wed another man. Did she love him more than you? Or did she hate you fervently? She laughed aloud. The whip died. The lightning ceased. The He-Ghoul is a man, but always and only a man. He can't stand comparison. Will never forgive being downgraded. Who can kill a man more easily than his wife? The fissures on the He-Ghoul's body widened. She became livelier. Whatever! Your wife is a very happy woman now. She has two children. She sold this bungalow. You do not exist even in her memories. You now exist only in the memories of your victims like me, what a joke!

As she watched, the He-Ghoul grew dim, dimmer. Please go away—his entreaty echoed in the room. She laughed again, satisfied. Yes, I will, she said, but some journeys have to be made alone.

She heard a car outside. The flames died down. The lights came on. The doorbell rang. She went up the stairs quickly, into the drawing room and opened the front door. From behind the sleepy-faced caretaker and his wife, her present lover stepped up, worry writ large on his face. Seeing her, he relaxed. As they shut the door and went up the stairs with his bag, he asked her again—Is everything okay? Didn't think you'd come, she said, delighted. She took him to the room in which her first lover had spent his last night. The lights went off again. The wind growled again. The trees moaned. The bats raged. The dogs bayed. The bungalow shook and shivered. He lay with her, unshaken, pressing his face into her shoulder. For her, sex and poetry were one and the same. If it did not touch with word and pith, she felt neither.

'Nice house,' he said. 'Why not stay on here?'

'Aren't you scared of the ghoul?'

'No, aren't we men all ghouls of the same old eroded masculine hubris?'

'Aren't you afraid of me?' she asked. 'Will any man love a woman who sleeps with her new lover in the bungalow where her old lover was killed?'

'In love, there is no man, no woman,' he said. 'Let us be free human beings.'

In the darkness, somewhere, something made of glass broke and scattered. The shards flew hither and thither. Without journeys, human beings will never be free. When she left that bungalow where her first lover was killed, she was not alone. Some journeys, of course, are not to be undertaken alone.

Translated from the original Malayalam
'Aan-Pretam' by J. Devika.

MONKEYS IN THE ONION FIELD

Kanishk Tharoor

**Kanishk Tharoor** is the author of *Swimmer among the Stars*, a collection of short stories that won the Tata Literature Live! First Book Award for fiction. He is the presenter of the BBC radio series *Museum of Lost Objects*. His essays on politics and culture have appeared in publications around the world, including the *New York Times*, *Guardian*, *New Yorker* and *Caravan*. He is a columnist for the *Hindustan Times* and the *Hindu BusinessLine*.

In her youth, Himani Devi had revelled in the smell of the onion fields in moonlight. She'd sneak out of home to meet friends, cousins, boys and, eventually, the young man who became her husband. Early on, Yash had taken her by the waist and lowered her beneath the hum of the insects. That sudden movement, so decisive and forceful, surprised her and surprised Yash as well, and they lay amid the onions, his body rigid with fear, barely daring to move his lips from where they rested on her cheek, a very timid gift. It was left to her to remove the glasses from his face and guide his mouth. She remembered that it was nearing harvest time that night. White and lilac petals drooped from the wilting onion stalks. As Yash nuzzled her breasts with his nose, she found herself imagining water coursing through the threads of the roots, up into the great reservoir of the bulb, where it seethed and tumbled, a river pulsing between the walls of the onion, frothing up through the stem until it met the air in an umbel of flowers.

But the older she got, the more perverse that smell seemed to her, its sweetness too insistent. Bipin, their only child, got fed up with their attachment to the village and its onion field. He had grown sick of scrabbling in the mountains. All his cousins and his friends, all the morose uncles and the muscular aunts, all of them had gone. On his last night, Bipin fought with Himani Devi and Yash, and tried to convince them to move down to the plains or to hill towns like sensible people. In the morning, Yash wept at the sight of his son in trousers, a burlap bag on his shoulder. Himani Devi asked Bipin to send what money he could, but not to sacrifice for them; he should live his life fully, he was doing the right thing.

Why won't you leave, Mother, why won't you leave? Bipin was disconsolate. There's the house, she replied, as if their one-room dwelling with its tin roof and windows patched with plastic was an immovable argument. And she nodded in the direction of the field. There are the onions. Bipin inhaled. He marvelled at the stubbornness of his parents—sometimes, the older we get, the more impermanent the world seems and the more things can be changed, matters altered. But not here. Promise you'll come during the holidays, Yash said. Bipin promised he would and left with the rising of the mist.

Within months, they received word that Bipin had fallen from a high scaffold, somewhere in another country, and died.

The village was so empty by then that only five others accompanied them in performing the funerary rites. In the absence of a priest—he was supposed to come from a nearby town but never showed up—they muddled through and improvised as best they could. Yash fretted that they had done an insufficient job, that their son hadn't been sent off properly. Himani Devi didn't have the strength to disagree; she had fooled herself for years believing that she was one of the lucky mothers who never ever had to let their child go.

The thought of leaving grew even more distant. Leave to go where? To whom? Former neighbours and distant relatives, all urged them to come down from the mountains. They refused. When their last neighbour left, they roamed up and down the path as if in a daze, wondering if a village without people was still a village. But their solitude was not something to fear or regret. What world could there be for them beyond their own? It didn't seem right that they might live elsewhere, that without ever wanting it for themselves they might live a life denied to their son.

———

The monkeys came into the onion field only at night, out of respect for their vocation as thieves. It was too brazen, even for them, to rummage for bulbs during the day. By the time the sun rose, the monkey clan had wandered back to the trees, whispering to each other and passing onion gruel into the mouths of their babies. Himani Devi limped out of the cottage and thought for an instant that all was well, that nothing had happened in the night. The field was grey and shapeless, as grey and shapeless as she had left it at dusk. But then she stepped on broken stalks and spotted tufts of hair on the ground where two monkeys had wrestled, and she realized that she had allowed herself to be robbed yet again.

It was the third time in as many weeks. Himani Devi had raised onions all her life, and never before had they invited the persistent ravages of monkeys. She scolded the scarecrow. Why didn't you stop them, she said. Always just standing there doing nothing . . . You're useless. The scarecrow swayed slightly at the reproach, aggrieved, as if to say: What

23

do you take me for, a scaremonkey? Annoyed, she stripped the scarecrow of its hat and thwacked it on the arm. The dew sparkled in the sunlight, showing Himani Devi the patches where the monkeys had performed their most committed excavations. She calculated the loss in terms of packets of biscuits and cups of tea, and came to the conclusion that she might have to go a week without her afternoon sweet. The forest sloped up the hills from her plot of land, mist hanging from the trees, a cloud settling on the wreck of a once-hopeful signal tower. Somewhere in the rousing green of the valley, there were monkeys making a rogue breakfast from her onions.

She replaced the hat on the scarecrow, suddenly feeling a bit sad for its threadbare pate. It wore a ragged sweatshirt that her son had left behind and never returned to. Yash called from the cottage to ask for hot coals for his hookah. She hobbled to the brazier at the front of their home, where a few embers still burned low. Up and down the main path, every window was boarded up, every door padlocked, every wall peeling. The only life in the hamlet was in their home where her husband Yash scratched himself in the doorway and knelt over the hookah to prepare his morning smoke.

The damn monkeys, she told her husband, please do something about them. Yash lifted his face upwards to the clouds, from where all his wife's requests seemed to descend. What can I do about monkeys? His voice was vaporous, not yet thickened to its usual fog. She plucked the glasses from his face and began to rub them with the end of her pallu. They're eating our onions, she said, I won't have it. He blinked at her and his enormous Adam's apple shifted mutely. He looked at his hands. I couldn't kill them, he said. She shook her head in agreement. It went without saying that nobody else would kill them either. Some years ago, there were still people living in their village, people of various ages, even little boys who might be tempted to patrol the fields with sticks for the promise of a few coins. They had all gone, disappeared to the plains or to the cities. The labour of others was now a remote idea, almost unfathomable to Himani Devi and Yash in their isolation. If the facts of the world could be changed, only they would change them.

———

Monkeys were a difficult kind of fact. Farmers across the region had a range of techniques for keeping the creatures away. There were chemicals that you could spray around the border fences. Poorer farmers used dried fish instead, which drove monkeys to such madness that they would rub themselves until they bled. The poorest farmers rolled balls of rice in heaps of chilli powder and scattered them around the edges of the field. Scathed, their tongues on fire, the monkeys would retreat to forage elsewhere.

Himani Devi and Yash could not afford any of these defences. They rarely ever had enough rice for themselves, never mind the laying of spicy landmines. Pesticides were used in the village in the past, but were now entirely out of reach, both too expensive and too far away. With no neighbours to borrow from, Yash would have to walk over fifteen kilometres to the nearest village, from where he'd catch a sporadic bus to the market town, where he'd have to hope that the old vendor would remember him and sell the chemicals on credit. His wife didn't begrudge him avoiding this unlikely quest.

They didn't have dried fish either, nor did either of them have the wherewithal to catch fish in the high streams. In any case, Himani Devi found something horrific in the thought of incensed monkeys scratching themselves raw under the flowering stalks of her onions.

Instead, wife and husband settled on devising a ruse. Himani Devi recalled a practice from the next valley, where farmers dangled multicoloured rubber hoses around their fields. The hoses would hang like snakes on a branch, stirring in the mind of an invading monkey a deep, immemorial fear.

Of course, Yash and Himani Devi didn't have spare hoses themselves. Perhaps there are old hoses in the neighbours' homes, she said. Yash squatted and flexed his toes with their black-and-blue nails. We shouldn't steal, he said. Himani Devi sighed, at once annoyed and warmed by her husband's loyal melancholy. We're just borrowing them . . . After the harvest, you can put them back.

They spent the rest of the morning scavenging. Yash approached their neighbours' homes politely, as if he were an unwanted guest. Though padlocked, many doors had rusted off their hinges and it was just a matter of pushing. In other places, they could open the shutters and clamber through the windows. It was odd picking over the remains of their neighbours' belongings. To be fair, both of them had done this several times in previous years in search of tobacco or medicines or spoons. But it never ceased to feel like a violation.

On his way out of a dust-filled home where birds sparred under the shingles, Yash apologized to a doorpost.

His wife rummaged farther down the path. Yash leant against a wobbly fence and inhaled the descending mist. It bothered him that he no longer remembered which house belonged to which family. When the village was full, or even half-full, neighbours were to be gossiped about and lamented. How loud she plays her radio; he lets his goat eat our spinach; she looks at me with such a jealous stare; why do they have to dress their children so well, it makes the rest of us look bad. In their absence, Yash felt sorry for all the times he had spoken ill of them to his wife, all those moments every day when his wife, peering out the window, would shake her head and snort. If they hadn't been so snide—even in secret—perhaps some of the others might have stayed.

Himani Devi's search turned up three rubber hoses—all in ratty condition, but they would pass as snakes. With the lines slung over her back, she struggled on to the path and called to Yash for help. He did not answer. She called out again. For a moment she entertained the helpless fantasy of being truly alone. But it was an articulated silence, the kind of silence she was sensitive to after decades of life together, a silence in which she felt his blood moving. She came to a doorway and saw him squatting inside the front room of somebody's abandoned home, holding a hairbrush.

Why are you crying? she asked and dabbed at the tears slipping down the creases of his face. Yash looked at her with his mouth open, gulping a sob. Don't you remember this brush? Himani Devi did remember it. For some people, a lifetime of hairbrushes may hardly be worth the space of their remembering, but for Yash and Himani Devi, the objects they gained and kept were fairly precious. Each was more than just an instrument, it was a claim to belonging in the world which, up in their mountains, could otherwise seem so tenuous and on the verge of dissolving.

It had been her hairbrush years before, a chip of the plastic missing from the handle. When she managed to get a replacement, Bipin had taken it. He picked every last strand of hair from its bristles and gave it to the girl who had lived in this now empty house. Himani Devi remembered her son's return after gifting the girl this brush, the shy hidden smile, how he couldn't control the energy of his limbs. She had sent him to tend to the field. With the sun setting, she'd watched Bipin skip around the onion rows, swatting away invisible enemies with a stick, each thin motion of his body brimming with laughter.

Himani Devi released Yash's fingers from the brush and enfolded her husband in her arms.

———

The human village once glowed with the heat of many lives. Now it is cold and empty. From the perspective of the monkeys, there seems to be little dividing the hamlet from the surrounding hills. The jungle has already retaken those houses on the outskirts, their fields and gardens, once so militantly kept, now overgrown. A few homes are topless, roofs caved in. Blackness calls through the windows. Only in one place, at the heart of the village, are there humans. The light of a gas lamp struggles to reach out of the door and on to the ambling back of an old female. She picks through the lines of her crop, fingering the green shoots. The monkeys watch her without making a sound. She straightens and looks at the stars, the dull moon and, many valleys away, the faintest haze of other humans. When she returns to her home, the monkeys wait for the lamp to be blown out. Then the order is given, the parents release their grips on the tails of the young, and the whole troop comes out of the forest, alive to the sweet, perverse smell of onions.

Later, up in the trees, one monkey hoards his cache of onion shoots. Others soon notice that he has not consumed his share. They pester him, chucking old fruit at him, besieging him with suggestions. When dealing with their own kind, most monkeys, like most humans, are good-natured, and see force as a last resort. They try to persuade him. You can't possibly eat so much, they explain, why keep all those onions to yourself? He bats them away and climbs to a higher branch. You look ridiculous, they say, you can't even swing properly, what with those onions clutched between your hands and feet, squeezed under your armpits. He snarls at them and attempts to move to another tree, but encumbered as he is, he stumbles, and his onions fall to the ground. Monkeys below whoop with glee and gather them up to feast.

Chastened, he retreats higher, to the canopy, holding with two hands the only onion left to him. The bulb is young and tough, the shoot thin. It will hardly do, he thinks, what a terrible gift. All creatures have powers of imagination, and with his, he has dreamt of impressing the young monkey he wants as his mate; he will give her a stack of onions. He thrusts his head above the line of leaves and branches, feels the sunlight cut through his eyes and drum on the top of his head. He cannot fight for her, he has a modest and wholly self-aware sense of his chances. Other monkeys are bigger, other monkeys are stronger, other monkeys delight in the pell-mell of the scrum. But perhaps with a significant donation, she might look at him with her watery eyes, turn her back, and let him lift up her tail.

He eats the onion, which is hard like a pebble. Monkeys do not always have long memories. Tonight, he resolves, tonight I will forage for my mate.

He leads the assault. The other monkeys are surprised by his bravado; normally he's more the shrinking sort. But the moon is a sliver and the stars drowsy and for once the darkness doesn't mock the monkeys with its terrors, but resolves around them like armour. He can smell the onions now and picks up the pace, a battalion scampering and clambering behind him.

The dangling form of a rubber hose gives him only a moment's pause. He studies its length, and cannot see its head, coming to the conclusion that it is probably a vine or some kind of creeper, not a python. He turns and calls out to his companions. Watch out for the snakes! This will slow them down, he thinks, more onions for me.

The human female has abandoned her post and gone off inside her dwelling. The monkey knows the scarecrow isn't real, some kind of frozen, immobile, perfectly useless being. He rolls into the line of crops. The earth smells wet and he presses his nose to the ground and hears the thrum of water coursing and insects shifting and faintly, almost imperceptible but still loud enough to the monkey, the sighs of onions growing old. He begins to dig. The treasures come out one by one, white heads with long green beards and the dreadlocks of roots. He amasses them in a pile. Other monkeys arrive nearby. Such a liar, they call to him, you can't have this field all to yourself.

They grow silent. He sees a human foot—it is attached to a human leg. Then another leg, and then the whole body of a man moves through the onion field. The monkey backs away, scrambling for his onions. He notices the smell; the human has none.

The human glows. When the monkey summons the courage to look up, the human's face is a dark swirling cloud, as if smoke could tumble from empty air. But then it changes, hardening into the face of a young man with very white teeth and plump eyebrows. He looks down on the monkey and smiles. With impossible speed, the young man's arm swings downwards, and the monkey feels the hand pass through his chest like a cold wind.

The other monkeys yell and flee to the forest. Again, the man's head turns into a black nimbus, bolts of lightning flashing around its edges, and the monkey feels himself rising, as if lifted by a gale that brings him level with the man's cloud-head. A boy's face emerges from the murk. What kind of human is this, the monkey begins to wonder, but can no more, his monkey mind overwhelmed with a flood of human images and smells: bread forked straight out of a tandoor, a father wetting and combing his son's hair, a mother massaging her

KANISHK THAROOR

son's little feet with eucalyptus oil, the parted lips of a girl, fireworks in a bright village, the damp of the onion field under a full moon, a desert—unfathomable to the monkey, but now so clear—with dunes wavering away to the horizon, a tree of steel beams and scaffolds, and then the broken harness and slipped line, and the shattering fall that the monkey feels now as an echo, a ripple of some distant and immense pain reaching up and down his hairy monkey body.

He tumbles to the floor and without looking back runs to the forest. When at last the panic releases its hold over him, the monkey climbs up a tree and gazes down on the field. He cannot see any human there, only the motionless form of the scarecrow. Even monkeys can experience incredulity. He hangs from the branch, staring over the forest, uncertain if he'll ever want an onion again.

Yash rose before Himani Devi that morning. She had tossed and turned during the night and, without meaning to, slept in long after sunrise. She blinked awake to find her husband standing over her with a cup of tea. Come, he said, I want to show you something. He led her outside. Himani Devi could already sense that the monkeys had visited again in the night, that the rubber snakes had failed. But there was a calming lightness in Yash's manner that made her curious.

He guided her into the centre of the field. Look, he pointed at the base of the scarecrow. I'm hardly awake, what is it? she said. Look, just look. He squeezed her wrist and they knelt by the pile of dug-up onions. After all the nights of wanton pillage, the monkeys had simply abandoned their loot. Himani Devi laughed. If this is how the world repays me for my patience, she thought, so be it. She moved to sweep up the decorous onion mound, but Yash gasped. No, he stopped her, as if she was about to disturb something sacred, a strange gift from another world.

THE LAST TRYST

Shashi Deshpande

Shashi Deshpande is a novelist and short-story writer in English. She has written ten novels, a large number of short stories, four books for children and many articles, some of which have been put together in the anthology *Writing from the Margin*. She has also done translations from Kannada and Marathi into English. Her novel *That Long Silence* won the Sahitya Akademi Award (1990). She was awarded the Padma Shri in 2009.

There she is, yet again, in the midst of the crowd. I sense her presence the instant I enter the hall. Each time she comes, she sits in the same place. She never moves, staying where she is, quiet, unmoving, her face in the shadows, which gives her a veiled look. So far she has not approached me. Which is strange, because all those who come here want something from me. They come with appeals for justice, they come with complaints, some of them come only to see me so that they can go back to their village and tell everyone that they saw the king. And some come with little gifts, gifts which speak of their love. But this woman has not asked for anything; she has not brought me anything, either. In fact, she has not shown any desire to meet me.

The first day I saw her, I was curious. This is not a place where women come, not by themselves, and never without a man. Seeing her in the midst of men, I was uneasy, anxious for her. More, because in the last few months, the atmosphere has been one of anger and belligerence. Men have been loud and angry in their complaints, in their accusations against one another. The discord between them has been open, each trying to shout down the others. I had thought, then, of asking my guards to take her out of here, to take her to the queen. But even as I framed the thought in my mind, she was gone. No, not gone—she disappeared, as if she had dissolved.

The next time she came, she stayed longer and I saw that she was untouched by the men around her, by their aggressiveness and their shouts. It seemed as if she knew she was safe; she was like an island of tranquillity in a stormy sea. I left her alone after that. If things between the queen and me had been the way they were earlier, I would have talked to her of the woman, asked her to speak to the woman, to find out why she was here and what we could do for her. But things have changed between us since I came back from the war. At first she comforted me, she cried over me, she wept for the dead, for our friends and kinsmen, she wept most of all for Abhimanyu, my sister's son, she wept over the fate of his young bride. And then, sensing that these were things I could not talk about, things I did not want to talk about, she left me alone. And I too began visiting her less. How could I go to her rooms, so full of the innocent joys of a woman and her children, carrying my nightmares inside me? How could I tell her that every night I am tormented by ghosts who won't leave me alone? There have been times when I wake up from these dreams, my sleep broken by my own sobs. Or so I think, but my face is dry. Sometimes, I wake up to the sounds of my shouts, my frightened cries. Do I want her to be a witness to these things? To her, I am still the man she flew to with the courage of innocence. The man she came to with the directness with which a bird goes to its nest. If she sees what I have become, what will it do to her, how will she live? No, I know I cannot lay the burden I am carrying on her.

Now it is only me and my ghosts. More than seeing them, I hear them, I hear the anguished cries of the dying, the lamentations and loud wails of the bereaved, when, searching the battlefield for their sons, their husbands, their fathers, brothers, their friends and lovers, they finally find them. I want to stop my ears against their wails, but I can hear them in spite of that. Sometimes, in my dreams, I am the one who is going around, searching for someone, my feet slipping in blood. I look at faces, I turn over the bodies when they are lying prone. As if this is a duty I have to perform, I keep going from body to body, searching. I can never find the person I seek. And then I wake up and the ghosts are still with me, they have not gone, their din filling my ears to the exclusion of everything else.

I am weary, I am weary of the ghosts who come to me in the night, I am tired of the duties I have to go through during the day. These last few days, the control I had over men seems to be slipping away from me. They no longer listen to me, they go on with their arguments and their quarrels as if I am not here. There was a time when a look, a word from me, would have sufficed. Even now, my guards look at me hopefully, expecting me to give them the command which will put these men in their place. How can I? I have no right to command anyone. It is I who am responsible for what is happening here, I who opened the large chest of hate, anger and jealousy when I encouraged the beginning of the war. I was so certain I was right, so sure that it was my duty to correct whatever was wrong. My decision, I was convinced, was the right one. My brother was the one person who told me I was wrong. 'There will be war,' he said. 'I can see it coming. But don't take sides, they are all our kin. Keep away from their quarrels.'

How could I? Those five brothers were tied to me not only by the bonds of kinship, they were my friends. And besides, the oldest brother was the right man to rule the kingdom. Wise, gentle and far-seeing, who could be a better king than he? As for the arrogant, callous man whom the old king supported only because he was his son, no one could be a worse ruler. He saw nothing beyond his own desires and his glory, no one but himself. He did not understand that ruling was not about your own power and glory, it was about the good you could do for others. No, I could not let such a man become king. I had to be on the side of right.

I tried to tell my brother this, I promised him that I would never fight myself. 'You don't have to fight,' he said. 'Just to know that you are with them will give them the courage to fight.' Finally, seeing that he could not make me change my mind, my brother left. On a pilgrimage, he said. But I knew it was to get away. He did not want to see what was going to happen. But he could not escape it entirely; he came back in time to see the end of the war, he saw the last battle being fought. The man who had been so drunk on power, so sure he would defeat his enemies and become king, he was the only one left. His friends, his brothers, all the warriors he had been so proud of and boasted about—they were all dead. He had walked away from the battlefield, he had laid down his arms and refused to fight. They called him a coward, but I knew that, whatever he was, he was no coward; he was finally seeing the truth, the truth that comes to a man when he has lost everything. But he was a warrior. Goaded and provoked, he came back to fight with his most bitter enemy. I admired him in that moment. He knew it was over, but he fought with the same ferocity with which he had always fought. Though, this time there was desperation as well. I saw him for the first time as a tragic figure. And when, finally, he lay on his back, his life flowing out of him with his blood which collected in a pool under his body, my brother looked at me. It was as if he was asking me: Are you happy? Is this what you wanted? Have you got what you wanted?

It began then, the question hammering in my mind: What have I done? What have I done?

It was the moment we had waited for, the moment we had fought for. But nobody, not even I, had imagined it would be so bitter, so terrible. We had to go and see the king, we had to tell him all his sons were dead. I had to go with the five brothers. I had been with them through the war, through the decision-making. Now I had to be with them to face the parents of the men we had defeated, the men we had killed.

Nobody announced us. There were no people left in the palace to do their duties, they were all out on the battlefield searching for their wounded, their dead. Yet the king raised his head as soon as we entered. With the uncanny ability of the blind, he seemed to sense our presence. Or did he smell the blood of his sons on us? The oldest brother, never a coward in such matters, went straight to them—yes, the queen was also there—and, folding his hands, began. 'King . . .' he said.

'I am not the king,' the man, who had never been swift with his retorts, said at once. 'You are the king. This throne is yours, the palace is yours. Everything is yours.'

Everything? What was this everything?

There was silence. And then the queen spoke—she spoke not to the brothers who had been wronged by her sons, not to the brothers who had killed her sons, but to me. 'Your family will be destroyed, they will destroy themselves,' she said. Was it a curse? She had said it quietly, without any anger. I could say nothing.

We went away from the palace, I left the place and came back home. I had my own kingdom, my duties, my work. I would put away the past and fulfil my obligations towards my own people. It was after I came home that the haunting began and my nights became full of the ghosts of the people I thought I had left behind. All night I heard the agonized cries of the wounded and the dying, I heard the lamentations of the living. And there was the silence of the dead, which to me was the loudest sound of all. Their silence, their closed eyes, were worse than the cries and reproachful looks of the others. They are the only people left in my life now, these ghosts who seem more real than the people I live among.

And, for the last few days, there is this woman who appears in my hall, the woman who has never spoken to me, never even looked at me. But for some reason, I think that she is on my side, I think she understands what I am going through. When I look at her, I forget the angry, quarrelling men in the hall and a sense of peace enters me. It is as if I am taken back to the years of my childhood, of my boyhood, back to the village where I lived the early years of my life. Most humans think of their childhood as the best days of their life. I had so much more reason than most to think that way. I was loved as few children are. It was a charmed life, with nothing coming in the way of my freedom, my pleasures. And there were my friends, boys who admired me and followed me blindly. No, there was nothing lacking in my life.

Yet, as I was growing up, I could feel a confusion within me. A sense of being someone else, of belonging somewhere else. Knowing, in some strange way, that though I was one of the village boys, I was different from them. I had a feeling that my real life lay outside that small village. I felt in myself a capacity for larger deeds, for greater actions than what was possible there. I had to get out. And then I would think of my parents, of my friends, of all the love that almost drowned me. There was only one person to whom I could talk of these things. I had not noticed her at first, but as I grew up and got to the age when I found girls fascinating, I saw her, not only because she was a girl, and a beautiful one, but because of the way she looked at me. There was something in that look which took away some of the confusion. We began meeting quietly on our own. With her, I found pleasures that I did not know existed in this world, I found a person who seemed to be part of me. There was nothing I could not talk to her about. I could speak to her of my greatest hopes and ambitions, of my greatest fears, of the confusion within me. Of the feeling that though this was my home, I did not belong here. And how disloyal and guilty I felt thinking that way.

She listened to me quietly, not saying much. She did not laugh, or even smile, when I told her I wanted to become great, that I knew that one day I would be among the greatest. She took me seriously, she made me feel she understood what I was saying. Be patient, she advised me, your time will come.

And then the messenger came from Mathura. My brother and I had been invited by the king. We had to go. I was full of joy, my destiny had finally beckoned me. The village rejoiced for us, the village mourned our going. They comforted themselves with the thought that we would soon return. But looking at the way the messenger behaved with my brother and me, I had my doubts. Why was he treating us as if we were royalty? I got a glimpse of my identity then, of the future I had only dreamt of and imagined. And I began to understand that my future was not there, in that village. And that, in my future the little village had no place.

I did not voice any of these thoughts. I immersed myself in visiting everyone, in saying farewell to everyone. And then, it was time for us to leave. The villagers followed us, they were reluctant to turn back. The king's messenger thought they were worried about us, he assured them that we, my brother and I, would be safe, that he would look after us as if we were his own children. When we came to the boundaries of the village, my brother stopped, turned round and folded his hands, as if he was telling them, 'Go back.' They stopped, suddenly, where they were. I had turned round too and as I looked at them, I had an inkling that I would never see them again. And then I saw her, standing with the women, but a little apart, so that I could see her clearly. I had not met her when I went around visiting everyone; in fact, I had not looked for her. I raised my hand to her, trying to tell her I was sorry. She understood, because she smiled, a smile that seemed to say, 'It has come for you, the call you were waiting for. Go, go now and meet your destiny.'

I walked away. How easily I walked away! There was a small pang of regret, but the future lay ahead of me and I walked towards it with eagerness and confidence.

We never went back to the village. I sent my trusted and loyal men later, when my brother and I had done what we had to and installed our father on the throne. I sent messages and gifts to the village with these men. I had no time to go myself, there was so much I had to do. I will go some time, I thought. But the time never came. I got caught up as a king in the stranglehold of power, embroiled in the petty rivalries of petty rulers, in plots and intrigues and alliances. I was busy making a name for myself, which I did so well that soon my name was on everyone's lips. The village receded and so did the innocent boy I had been. And the girl who had asked nothing for herself, who had only wanted me to get what I wanted, I forgot her too.

Now, seeing the woman in my hall, I am reminded of her, I am reminded of those days of innocence. Why did I think she has brought me nothing? She has brought me the gift of memories, memories of the boy I had been. The most priceless gift of all. Memories that tug me away from the ghosts who so tirelessly haunt me. I remember how, at times, at the end of the day, like all boys reluctant to end the day, to go home, we lingered. As twilight fell, our mothers' voices floated to us through the quiet of the evening, high and anxious, and yet sweet, like birds in the evenings when they get to their nests. But we still put off going home, we sat in a circle and told one another stories, stories of ghosts, each one bringing out a story more frightening and horrifying than the others'. We spoke of ghosts with no heads, ghosts with two heads, ghosts with hideous bodies and ugly faces, ghosts with long nails and sharp teeth. I did not know then, none of us did, that the most fearful ghosts are not those with distorted faces and grotesque bodies, but men and women like us. People we have wronged. They come to us in the night and stand before us, asking, 'What have you done to me? What have you done?' They ask me, 'Did you think that you could fight a war, kill and maim, destroy families and find the world unchanged at the end of it?' They ask, 'Did you think you could put the demons of anger and jealousy back into the box after you had let them loose?' I can see the demons here, in this hall, fluttering among the men I thought I knew so well, turning them into angry, violent strangers.

At times, I wonder whether we could have done something else, something different. I wonder whether, if I had not been on their side, the brothers would have gone to war at all. Then again I tell myself I was not the only guilty one, that all of us on both sides were guilty. And yet, why was it so important that we do our duty, the duty of fighting? Could we not, for once, have refused to do this duty? And why did I, who as a child had known neither his identity nor his duty, give it so much importance? Why had I embraced this duty with greater fervour than the others? Futile questions which are pointless today.

I look around me at the men who are becoming more and more belligerent. Their warlike gestures, the aggressive language they are using—gestures and language which had been part of my life earlier—seem grotesque to me now. I am full of shame that I too had once been the way these men are now. I should stop them, I should do something, but I can no longer make myself act or speak. My guards, tired of waiting for my commands, have begun trying to separate the men, they are pushing them out of the hall. In a while they are gone, pursuing one another, my guards chasing all of them. There is nobody left in the hall except me. And the woman. I look at her and I see her for the first time, her face clear and out of the shadows. Even without seeing her face, I know who she is. I call out her name. She smiles at me, the same smile she had given me when I was leaving the village, a smile that said, 'Go and meet your destiny.' I raise my hand to her in farewell, as I had done all those years ago when I left the village. And then she is gone, not out of the room, like the men; she disappears, she dissolves, as she always does.

It no longer matters to me. I know what I have to do. I walk out of the hall with the sure steps of a man who knows where he is going. There are still a few men milling around, some of them fighting with their bare hands. I go past them. In the distance I can see the sea glimmering in the sunlight, the sands white and shining. I can see some men there. I know ultimately they will all go there, where there is more room for them to fight. I walk away from them, away from the sea, and make my way to the grove of trees some distance away. I can no longer hear any sounds; there is perfect silence here. I reach a spot where the trees are so close that not a ray of sunshine can enter. *This is the place*: I hear the words in my mind and lie down under a tree, my head pillowed on my arms. I close my eyes and wait for her to come to me. The last tryst.

IN A SMALL ROOM, SOMEWHERE

Jerry Pinto

Jerry Pinto has won the National Award for Best Book on Cinema for *Helen: The Life and Times of a Bollywood H-Bomb,* and the Hindu Lit for Life Award, the Crossword Award for Fiction and the Sahitya Akademi Award for his novel *Em and the Big Hoom.* He won the Wyndham Campbell Award administered by the Beinecke Library at Yale University in 2016. He has translated five books into English from Marathi: *Cobalt Blue* by Sachin Kundalkar, *I, the Salt Doll* by Vandana Mishra, *Baluta* by Daya Pawar, *I Want to Destroy Myself; A Memoir* by Mallika Amar Shaikh and *Half-Open Windows* by Ganesh Matkari. He lives and works in Mumbai, which often scares him.

I used to read a lot of horror fiction, Dottoressa. I cannot tell a lie. When the monster from the depths of hell got his slimy paws on Tiffany the Disposable . . .

Oh Dottoressa, Dottoressa, surely you know Tiffany. You should know Tiffany. Especially if you want to understand me. What's that French saying? *Tout comprendre, c'est tout pardonner.* To know all is to forgive all, if you'll pardon my French. Tiffany is the blonde who can't act but who is buxom enough to look good in a negligee and who will go out into the dark night when she has been expressly told not to. That's Tiffany. She's so popular with the underworld that they have a bar called Breakfast at Tiffany's. Sorry, my little joke.

When Tiffany the Disposable gets hers, I get mine. You do know what I mean, Dottoressa. I reach into my pants for my cobra and I lure him out of his hood . . .

Ha, you winced. I got past the mask of impenetrable calm and non-judgemental rationality that you were trained to put on in Trick Cyclist School. You're no Clarice Starling. You're a bird of another feather altogether. You're a stool pigeon, you're a pigeon with stools all over her feathers . . .

Okay, I'm sorry, let me backtrack.

I'm innocent, Dottoressa, I'm innocent. It was those horror movies and horror stories that did this to me.

I want the truth to be told about my life.

I want you to know that horror stories might have been the saving of me.

And of all those people they called my victims.

I was happy enough being scared shitless. And I mean shitless. I would sit on the pot in our home—where else is a boy to do his snake-charmer act in a tiny Mumbai flat—and I would pretend to be straining when I was staining. And I was happy.

Then Mrs T—let's just call her that, Mrs T, my class teacher—found me with *Tales from the Crypt* and she said, 'How will you get ahead in life? You had better read the papers.'

I was an impressionable young lad then, Dottoressa, and I changed my ways. I turned to the newspaper and what do you think I found? I found that the world is a glorious, perfect horror story. It is all about horror.

I could not believe it.

When Ashley was fourteen months old, her mother put her into a searing oven.

Fact.

When Mirabelle was two months old, her mother put her into a microwave and killed her.

Fact.

When Olivia was four years old, her father drowned her in a baptismal pool.

Fact.

(I don't know her real name so I named her Olivia; it was not disclosed in the reports. Sorry about that, Dottoressa.)

When Brianna decided to smother her two-month-old baby, she shot a selfie video.

Fact.

Romechia kept swinging her son on a swing—swing, baby, swing—for three days, until he died of hypothermia and dehydration.

Fact.

You know the problem with fact, Dottoressa? There is no getting away from it. It is there. It is here. It is everywhere. It cannot be denied. There is no shutting the book, no turning off the movie and going off to make yourself a nice cup of cocoa. Wherever you go, you're in the middle of reality. Oh, of course, you're going to say: Last night I slept and dreamt I was a butterfly. How can I be sure I am not a butterfly who is asleep and dreaming he is a man?

I hope I am.

You should too.

Look around you. Remember that butterflies feast on carrion. That's dead flesh. They love urine. Collectors use it to trap them all the time. Serve the ammoniaphiles right. They love blood and shit too. When Master Zhuangzi dreamt he was a butterfly, did he dine, do you think? Ha ha.

So if this is a dream a butterfly is having, you can bet it's been eating some good stuff last night. That might be why we're living in this horror, living in it and no way to turn it off, no way to get out of it, no way to free yourself from the threat that they'll come for you.

This is the country, by the way, Dottoressa, that burnt a man and his nine-year-old child to death in a car.

Fact.

So what could I do, Dottoressa, what could I do?

I tried to retreat into reading again. I tried to go back to the old innocence of black words on a white page conjuring up incarnadine deeds and green slime. I tried and I found that I could see straight through them.

I could see their struts and I could see their props. I could see how the writers themselves were in retreat. I could see how they were lily-livered too and how they were trying to ignore reality. Could any of them imagine getting angry when their girlfriend made them dinner, and since they were not hungry, stomping out of the house, getting drunk and then coming back and raping their girlfriend's mentally challenged and mute daughter?

Fact.

You see, Dottoressa, they're writers. They're people who talk shit about the magic of words and how worlds can be summoned up by just so many letters and so many symbols and some well-arranged spaces between them.

They can't look into the abyss. When they do, the abyss starts looking into them and they turn away, afraid.

It was all pallid stuff. Yes, yes, Tiffany is eviscerated on page three after a suitably long time wandering around with lots of short sentences. You know?

The sound again. 'Who is it?' Tiffany asked. Her voice sounded thin in the darkness. Thin and afraid. 'Chin up, girl,' she told herself. But again. Behind her? She whirled around. Ahead of her? No, not there.

I was yawning even when it turned out to be a vaginal vampire. I mean, come on. Have you read about what they do to girls on Delhi buses?

Or to a girl who is from the lower orders, who wears her nice new uniform and walks through the village in shoes? They raped and murdered her and then went after her family. Who could dream up this command to that girl's brother: Have sex with your mother or we will kill her? Has there been a Mogambo who could think that up? Has there been a Dr No like that? No, these were just ordinary boys from a village, all together, teaching *them* a lesson.

I would put my nose into the papers and what would I smell?

I would smell fear.

Everyone was afraid.

And here's the thing.

When I was reading the paper, I would think: he must have been really scared when . . .

Or she must have been really scared when . . .

But it might not have been the most scary moment of their lives, Dottoressa. They might well have been relieved. Okay, it's happening. It's over. It will get over soon.

Another way of looking at it, Dottoressa?

Is there any hierarchy to the amount of fear?

A ninety-year-old man is burnt to death for entering the wrong holy place.

How much fear does he feel as the burning begins?

The rationalist goes for a walk in the morning and a murderer turns up and shoots him.

How much fear does he feel as the gun is raised?

The man whom the serial killer has tied up.

How much fear does he feel?

Is there a measure? If a Helen can be a measure of beauty, can we have a Hannibal as a measure of fear?

Now, I'm going to let you in on a secret, Dottoressa. I am going to tell you that I was afraid. I was really, really afraid when I read the newspapers.

I found that I hated being afraid.

I also discovered: Fear is really another name for hate.

These are the real four-letter words, Dottoressa.

Hate.

Fear.

Kill.

Fuck, cock and cunt? They're beautiful words, about things that give us pleasure, from which new humanity flows, from which hope is born again and again as babies come flooding into the world.

Hate.

Fear.

Kill.

I could not live in fear so I chose to live in hate.

Which is why I joined the ranks of those who are to be feared.

I joined them because I would rather be the man with the *mashaal* outside than the man cowering in fear inside.

I covered up my fear with hate.

I shouted: Kill, kill, kill!

I know you hate me, Dottoressa.

I know you fear me.

But just calm down. Be brave now.

What I'm going to do won't hurt a bit.

THE DAAYAN'S CURSE

Ipsita Roy Chakraverti

Ipsita Roy Chakraverti is an author and researcher into old world cultures and civilizations and has introduced in India the true face of Wicca. She has spoken out against lobbies with vested interests who use superstition to harass and brand women *daayans* in India. She is the founder of the Wiccan Brigade and the Young Bengal Brigade. Her books include *Beloved Witch*, *Beloved Witch Returns*, *Sacred Evil: Encounters with the Unknown* and *Spirits I Have Known*.

Have you ever listened to the dry, cryptic rustle of leaves or the sighing of the wind? I mean really listened. Have you ever heard the measured tread of feet on corridors you knew were empty? How about the soft movement of silk on a vacant chair? It isn't always your imagination when you hear that knock or tentative tap on the door . . . and there is nobody out there.

What I am about to relate happened a few years ago. Some of my readers might have heard of the incident. I was in a small town in Purulia and had rented an old house for a few weeks. The area was quiet, rustic, surrounded by fields and yet had the necessary facilities if one drove a few miles into town. I was trying to complete the last chapters of my latest book and wanted the quiet of nature around me. The days were restful as I would stroll into the countryside and in the evenings I would sit in a corner room upstairs, which I had converted into a study, and write, turning in at about eleven, after a simple dinner of rice, lentils and vegetables cooked by Jhumri, a most loyal and efficient tribal woman who looked after my household needs. That particular night, I had sat up later than usual. I had not been able to work in the evening, due to some visitors who were passing by on their way to Adra and had dropped in to meet me.

It was well after midnight. The night was quiet—no, now that I think back on it, I would say it was eerily still. A table lamp dimly cast its glow on my desk. I looked at the timepiece on the mantel and saw the minute hand move to '2'. It was ten past one. For some unknown reason I felt uneasy. That was unlike me. As a rule, I'm a very practical, grounded person not given to flights of feeling. I decided to make myself a cup of coffee and finish my manuscript. I would have to go downstairs to the kitchen for the coffee, but never mind. I would switch on the lights on my way down. It would also give me a chance to check the windows and the bolts on the front door. Of course, I was aware that Jhumri was always very particular about locking up firmly before she left for her quarters about half a mile away. She would, with much respect and many apologies, call me downstairs, ask if there was anything else I needed and then exit through the kitchen door. While I put on the padlock from within, she would warn me again and again never to open that door to any summons till she thumped on it in the morning. She had a special way of knocking which told me it was Jhumri. That was our code.

Now, as I pushed back my chair and stepped towards the window, which overlooked an adjoining field bordered by gnarled old trees, I suddenly froze. Was I imagining things? Was I frightened of something I couldn't quite decipher? But there it was—a sudden, spine-chilling scream from the field outside my window. I can truly say that I have never heard such a cry before. I hope one day I can forget it. It was half human and half animal. It was a cry of terror, agony and grief. At first, I thought it was coming from an animal in tremendous pain. It continued in that vein for some time—half wailing, half pleading. I had a strange feeling that it was directed at me. Calling out to me. I hurriedly wrapped a shawl over my dressing gown and, stepping out of my study, switched on the landing lights and went downstairs as quickly as I could to try and find the night chowkidar. I had employed Bhim, an elderly, retired security guard, to come in every evening at eight o'clock sharp and keep watch till dawn. He had come to me highly recommended by my nearest neighbours, former zamindars, who till recently had lived about four miles away. Now they had sold their property in Purulia and moved to the city. Bhim was without a job at the moment so he welcomed the work I was offering him. He was a good man, reliable and with an honest face—I liked him. And so he sat downstairs on a cane chair every night, wandered around the compound at intervals and knocked his stick against the gate and the house every hour till dawn to show that all was well. Occasionally he would doze, but he had an internal radar which knew exactly what was going on. He also kept awake with the help of a small radio. He liked Hindi film songs. I did not object to this because on all counts, he was very alert.

'Bhim,' I called out. 'What was that scream about? Who was that?'

On seeing me, he hurriedly rose and, with his torch shining a thin strip of light, came shuffling towards me. He seemed not to have heard it. Guiltily, he looked at his little radio and quickly turned it off, appearing startled to see me at that hour. He looked genuinely concerned.

'Anything wrong, memsahib?' he asked. 'Is all well? *Sab theek aachhe?*'

'Yes, yes,' I replied hastily, 'but what about that scream? Who was it? Didn't you hear?'

He sheepishly pointed to the radio. 'Might have been this, memsahib. It might have been too loud. I am sorry.'

'It wasn't the radio. It was somebody crying out. I want to have a look at the field outside,' I told him. 'Will you bring your torch and accompany me?'

He seemed a bit frightened for just a second but then he was himself. 'Of course, memsahib. I'll just get the bigger torch from my bag.' He was with me in a trice.

'Come quietly,' I said, as he followed me with his wooden stick and torch, casting a beam of light ahead of us on the dark path. We crossed the paved compound and came to the iron gates where we stopped while he took out a bunch of keys from a leather pouch at his side. He fitted a big key into the lock, which hung from the gate, and it opened. He pushed the left wing of the gate and it creaked loudly as it swung back. We stepped out on to a dark patch of paving, lit dimly by a light set over the gate.

'This way, Bhim,' I said, breaking the ominous silence. 'Shine your torch on to the field on the left.' We walked a few yards in that direction, where the houses ended and the empty stretch of grass and field began. He hung back nervously. I took the torch from him and swung it around to cover the vacant ground. He appeared willing enough to let me do the exploring but I must admit, he stayed by my side, reluctant to leave me alone, even though he reminded me a few times that this was no place for me at this time of night.

Suddenly I saw it. A shrouded black shape which seemed to flit across a corner of the field. It stopped when it reached an old sturdy tree, turned its head towards me, even though I had no way to be sure that that was its head, and then disappeared into the mist which seemed to be rising from the water of a pond just beyond that.

'Quick, Bhim, quick,' I shouted. 'Did you see that? There was someone there. Perhaps the person who screamed. You must find out.'

To my surprise, Bhim had fallen behind me quite a way and looked petrified. I turned back to him and asked, 'What's the matter? Didn't you see that person wrapped in black? Have you ever seen that figure before?'

'No, n . . . no,' he stuttered. 'I don't know anything about it. Come away, memsahib. This is a dark place. It's not a good place to stand about.' Bhim suddenly seemed genuinely frightened. I turned to the pond again and cast the light of the torch to where I had last seen the figure. There was nobody and nothing there. Only the branches of trees swayed slightly. And the snapping sound of twigs as creatures of the night walked over them.

'All right,' I said, 'let's go back. But I heard the most blood-curdling scream coming from here. It was a human being. I am sure of it.'

Bhim didn't reply. He just huddled up in his khaki shawl and escorted me, almost hurrying me back to our gate. I returned the torch to him. He shut and locked the gate very carefully behind us. I thanked him for his trouble. He bowed his head and salaamed, saying it was his duty.

Upstairs in my study once again, I parted the curtains and looked upon the field—awash with darkness but with a light spray of moonlight here and there. The contrasts seemed heightened. The silence denser. And there she was, right under my window, looking up. The figure stood beyond the compound wall. A pale white face riddled with pain and humiliation. A black cloth covered her shoulders and framed her face. I could not make out the rest of her body in the dark but it seemed to be a part of the bushes and undergrowth in the field. I stared, trying to focus on what I saw. Were my eyes playing tricks on me? Then there was an eerie moaning and she raised two white hands, bleached and bony, towards me. The face was crumbling, white, skeletal, but covered with patches of earth. The next moment, the figure was gone. Disappeared before my eyes.

I peered and gazed around the field. I got a torch and, from where I stood at the window, swung its beam around in the dark. But there was nothing and nobody there. I was fairly convinced by now that what I had seen was an apparition. But whose? And what was it trying to convey to me?

This particular field I talk of had a sinister reputation. At one time it used to be cultivated but now lay fallow and baked by the sun. After sunset the area was lonely. There was a lane running by it. Not many people walked there after dusk. It was rumoured that during politically troubled times there were shootings and stabbings on this field and people lay buried here.

These thoughts stirred in my mind as I made ready for bed. I had locked up carefully downstairs, thoughts of coffee long forgotten. Suddenly my eyes fell on an ad in a newspaper which lay folded on my bedside table. I picked it up and looked at the picture by the light of the lamp on my table. It advertised a soon-to-be-released Hindi film, *Desh ki Daayan*, which allegedly dealt with the subject of witches. It showed three actresses in weird costumes. I had heard that the stance of the producer was that witches were known to be beautiful but were actually evil and that every residential building contained a daayan. How strange, I thought, that this particular piece of print should present itself to my eyes now. This film was going to make a superstitious mockery of an ancient branch of learning. And how tragic that even today, in our country, where woman were branded daayans and killed for it, film-makers were making money off superstition. How unfortunate the women in our country were. They were either treated as sex objects or as daayans. The strange thing was that the producer of the film was a woman. Did she have no compassion for her own sex? Or was money the only goal this woman had? On one hand, I had heard that before the shooting of the film she had rushed to the temple to ask the blessings of the goddess Kali so that the curse of the daayan would not descend on her, but apparently she cared nothing for the havoc that this film could wreak in a country where hundreds of women were killed in the name of 'witchcraft'. We were truly regressing to the Middle Ages in India . . .

Suddenly there was a tap on the window and the frame rattled. I was startled. There was no breeze or storm brewing. Who or what had made that sound? I stepped to the window to check the latch. It was firmly in place. Before I could turn away and retrace my steps towards the bed, the newspaper which had been lying on the table next to it suddenly rustled and slid to the floor. I felt a presence now. Something or someone had come into the room. This was the one who had been trying to get my attention tonight. The presence who had been out on the field. The spirit which had erupted in that unearthly scream. Was it the haunted or the haunter? What did it want from me? I had to find out.

I quietly picked up the paper from the floor and once again saw the picture of a woman, an actress who had consented to play a daayan. Her eyes were blank as they stared at me from the picture. Then they started turning dark, as if trying to cover some kind of guilt. It was as if she knew she was letting her gender down by propagating the myth of witchcraft on-screen. She had done it for material gains. But would she be exonerated from the guilt? Wouldn't the eyes of all those women tortured and killed for being witches in our country follow her and demand to know why she had done this? The film-maker had even said that daayans had their evil power tied up in their hair, in their plaits. Would the superstition in our country force women to cut off their hair?

I started to prepare for bed. I was aware that something other-worldly had a message to communicate but I also knew that I was not yet able to pick it up. The conditions and the time were not right.

The next afternoon I was to return to the city for a day to deliver a lecture on the ancient goddesses of Wicca to a certain academic group. As I got ready, I glanced out the window at the field and the trees beyond, wondering who or what I had seen in the early hours. The ground was sparsely tufted with grass and dappled with sun and shade. Branches of tall, leafy trees cast pools of cold darkness. I got my things together and prepared to go downstairs. At the gate I ran into Bhim, who seemed to be hanging around even though he had completed his shift and could have gone home by now.

'What is the matter, Bhim?' I asked.

'Nothing, memsahib. I was just talking to the day chowkidar, explaining his duties to him. He is new to the area.'

'Did you hear anything more last night?' I asked him directly, not giving him much chance to decide what to reply.

'No, no,' he said in a rush. 'Nothing, memsahib. There was nothing.' Bhim went decidedly pale.

'But I heard someone scream,' I said.

'Maybe these night foxes, memsahib. They howl and wail sometimes when the moon is out.'

'It was a human being, Bhim,' I insisted. Then, not wanting to prolong his apparent discomfiture, I called for my car and left.

That evening when I returned to Purulia, I felt a sombre quiet in the atmosphere. Jhumri had switched on the lamps in the living room but the corners seemed cloaked in shade. I walked into the bedroom. The curtains had not been drawn yet and as I switched on the lights they were reflected in the glass panes of the dark rectangular window. I drew the curtains and for some reason did not glance outside. However, I was sure somebody was looking up at me from the field.

That night an earthquake rocked the north-eastern part of the country and Kolkata and nearby districts experienced the tremors. I was asleep at the time but woke up feeling the bed beneath me shiver and tremble. Stray dogs howled from amongst the trees and crows started a raucous cawing. Amidst all this, I heard somebody laugh long and hard from the field. This time I was sure the voice was a woman's. It was laughter that was vicious and strident. It was a laugh which announced that the destruction had just begun. And that revenge was sweet.

Yesterday's newspaper still lay on my bedside table. I remembered the picture of the celluloid daayans I had seen on the entertainment page. Tonight as I switched on the bedside lamp I noticed the picture slashed with a cross in dark black. Who had done this? It was extremely strange. Nobody entered my room in my absence. My maid had strict orders. I called out to her and questioned her.

'Jhumri, I left this paper here in the morning. And now I find this black marking on it. Did you do this?'

She took the paper from me and looked genuinely startled. 'No, didi. Of course not. I never enter this room when you are not here. And nobody else has been here.'

I knew from her face that she was telling the truth. Jhumri was simple and straightforward. She was also a bit shaken by this occurrence. A bit confused. I told her to start making my dinner and, as I changed into more comfortable clothes, I wondered. A sudden thought struck me. Could it be that . . . I would call Bhim upstairs and talk to him, after dinner. He must have come for duty.

He came with a nervous knock on the door. He stood there looking as if he had been found out. I almost felt sorry for the man. 'It's all right, Bhim,' I assured him. 'I just wanted to ask you if you remember an incident that happened near here sometime ago. You have been living here for many years now.'

'Yes, memsahib. Many years now.' He sensed that I was about to ask him something he would rather not talk about. 'But my memory has grown weak. I am not young any more.'

I smiled to myself. 'Bhim, do you remember an incident that took place about three to four years back, when a young widow, who lived in a village near here, was accused of being a daayan? It was said she was a shape-shifter and changed herself into a wolf every night to prey on children. Some men attacked her. Do you remember? What happened to her afterwards?'

Bhim turned pale. It was obvious that he did not want to recall the incident. He was afraid of the consequences. Night watchmen are often witness to the worst atrocities against women. But fear for themselves and their families makes them look the other way. I felt this must have been so in Bhim's case as well.

Suddenly, there was the sound of loud, high-pitched laughter from downstairs and Bhim turned ghostly white. He looked at me, panic writ large on his face, before turning and running headlong down the stairs, wailing that he would never be forgiven. Never, ever. May God protect him.

That night there was a massive storm in the city and the districts. Wind velocity was furious. The wind screamed and howled like a soul in hell. Trees were flattened as the storm crushed them and uprooted them like playthings. The rain came down in white sheets after the wind had abated. This seemed to be a protest from the elements. First an earthquake here, then a series of them occurred in the country that summer. Where had the country gone wrong? I read somewhere that the maker of the film showing Indian women as evil witches was having serious trouble with distributors and the tax department. Justice works in strange, unexplained ways.

I wondered if the message I was receiving, the apparition I was seeing, was connected in any way with what had happened here not so long ago. I asked Jhumri about it and she related to me as much as she could remember.

———

Meera lived in a village in Purulia with her old father. It was just the two of them, tilling a small tract of land, growing potatoes and barely scraping together a living. Meera's mother had died when she was six. She had no siblings. The mud-and-brick dwelling they had constructed for themselves stood up well to the elements but it was not too secure. Firdaus often feared for the safety of his daughter. In a male-dominated society, there was no place for women. What would she do to protect herself as he grew older and more frail? How would she survive after he passed on? They were poor with just these few *kottah*s of land. How would she manage?

His fears were not unfounded. Local goons often leered at Meera and passed obscene comments when she walked by on the way to the bazaar. She kept her head covered and wore simple and extremely modest clothing which she stitched herself. But there was no end to the harassment. A young woman alone in this country seemed to be an object of lewd attention. When these men, standing at the corners of the bazaar or on roadsides, could not provoke her, they started getting aggressive. Those older stall keepers in the bazaar who had known Meera since childhood were afraid to come to her defence. They pretended they had not heard the comments or looked the other way and pretended to be busy with other customers. Meera did not tell her father all for she did not wish to worry him but he guessed that things were not easy for his daughter. In small, rural areas, where things were so close and ingrown, might often became right.

Meera's sorrows began to multiply when the ruffians started trying to touch her or pull at her dupatta as she walked past. They laughed and leered and passed comments about her body. One day, one of these culprits, cruder than the others, claimed to have known her closely, intimately. Meera whipped around. She could not take this any more. She had been fuming for a long time and had been miserable. Now she had to react. Death would be better than this constant humiliation. And her words spilt out at them. People gathered to listen and watch the fun. This is what her pursuers had been waiting for. They started calling her a *daini*, a witch. They said that they had been watching her for weeks because she showed 'evil' signs. Her evil was tied up in her long hair. They tried to pull it and she screamed. The goons laughed. Some of the onlookers walked away, not wanting to get involved. The tormenters claimed that children in their neighbourhood had fallen sick whenever she visited any of their houses. The gullible and the bored listened with interest. A few women looked scared, wondering if this girl really had the evil eye. The witch-hunt began in earnest.

Those oafs would lie in wait for her in secluded corners and quietly watch her from across the fields when she worked on her father's land. They stood silently and in groups of twos and threes. They made gestures to her and smiled. Meera felt hunted. She wondered who would help her. She knew it would be useless complaining to the authorities. She and her father were too poor and insignificant. To be taken notice of, one had to have clout or money.

One morning, her father suggested she take a short break in the city.

'Meera, my child,' he said. 'I know times are bad. I know the nuisance these people are creating. I want you to go away to Kolkata for a few weeks. My sister and her family live in a place near Garia. I shall give you the address. Take a local train to Howrah and then the bus to her place. You won't have trouble finding it. I shall write to her today.' And thus it was that Meera quietly went to the neighbouring station early one morning, when not many people were about, and from there took the train to Kolkata. She reached Howrah within a few hours and did not have much trouble locating her aunt's house.

Life was comparatively calm and peaceful for a few days. Her aunt Sabita was a quiet, soft-spoken woman who tried to look after her. She lived in two very small rooms with her husband and their two children, but they didn't mind Meera's staying with them. They knew it would be only for a few weeks and besides, Meera had brought a bag full of potatoes with her, rice and other gifts from the land. They believed in family ties. However, they started getting disturbed when a group of surly young men began hanging about the lane where they lived, keeping an eye on their flat. At first they weren't sure whether they were the targets—later it seemed too much of a coincidence that they were there whenever Meera happened to go out or look out the window. A few of the ruffians seemed to be posted on duty to keep an eye on their movements.

When Sabita's husband approached them and asked them who they were, they were obnoxious and rude, answering him in the foulest language. They did mention Meera, however, and said they were waiting to get the 'daini'. They also told Meera's uncle that she would bring bad luck to the house if they put her up for too long. Better to send her back to where she belonged. The goons obviously had links with her village and had been told about her whereabouts. They had been following Meera.

Sabita was supportive but she worried for her own children. She didn't want her family getting involved in any unpleasantness. Meera stayed the week and then decided to go back home. But she never reached home. Her father searched for her. He lodged a missing person's report. Inquiries were made for some days and when nothing turned up it was said that she must have gone away with somebody of her own volition. It must be remembered these people had no clout or influence.

———————

I talked to Bhim one evening. He was leaving the next day and returning to his native village in Malda. I asked him a question for the last time. 'Bhim, do you really not know what it is that roams the field on certain nights? Who it is?'

'I know, memsahib,' he replied. 'It is the woman they branded a daayan. She has cursed them.'

'What happened to her?'

'They say she was thrown off a running train. But nobody knows for sure. They say every neighbourhood has a daayan. Maybe that is why they did what they did. To stop the evil.'

I must have looked shocked for he tried to explain.

'That is what that film says, memsahib. I saw it in the hall. It was about daayans.'

'You believe all this rubbish, Bhim?' I asked him. 'Don't you think it is all superstition? Would you let a woman in your own family be killed if somebody called her a daayan?'

'No, no, memsahib. Of course not. But we are simple people. We are afraid. The fact is that . . .' he trailed off.

'What is it, Bhim? What do you know?' I persisted.

'Well, memsahib, some people say that Meera was not really pushed off a train. Some say she was taken off the train and hacked to death for being a daayan, and the pieces of her body are buried here, in this field . . . where you saw her. We are all to blame. We did nothing to protect her when the trouble started.'

I was quiet. The curse of the witch. The film-maker had said that she was going to go to the temple to remove from her head the curse of the daayan. Was she as guilty then as the people who had killed Meera? She was exploiting age-old superstitions that still beset the country. They had done it for lust and power. She was doing it for money and material gain.

Suddenly, I saw the black shrouded form standing there. By the front gate. She looked at me, bowed her head as if in acknowledgement and then seemed to glide away. I got the impression that she stopped once to look back through that black veil. She appeared glad that I knew her story. I might have been wrong but I felt that she was trying to convey that she was fighting alongside me. We understood each other. This country would be cursed unless and until its women were safe again. The storm would never cease.

FALLING

Jahnavi Barua

Jahnavi Barua is a writer based in Bangalore. Her first book, *Next Door*, was a collection of short fiction. Her second book, *Rebirth*, was shortlisted for the Man Asian Literary Prize and the Commonwealth Book Prize.

The rain was coming down in opaque sheets. From where I sat at the table in the corner of the shop close to the window, I could not see the main road any more. The grinding of cars making their way up the steep slope was not audible either. Occasionally, through the drumming of the rain on the tin roof, I could hear the fragmented sound of a car horn. Each time, I held my breath, waiting to see if the car would stop, if the door to the shop would open. Three hours now and no one had stepped in.

'More tea?' the shop lady—Violet, I think her name was—asked.

'Yes, please.' My fourth cup so far.

Mid-afternoon, but it was dark as night. Violet had turned on the lights in the shop and they filled the cramped space with a welcome warmth.

I watched Violet move around behind the counter. This was an old-fashioned corner shop with all the goods stacked in neat shelves at the back of the shop. No self-service here: anything the customer wanted was handed over by Violet, who owned the shop, or her niece, a friendly young woman I had occasion to meet once or twice. The table in the corner and the cup of tea, often served with a quarter plate of glucose biscuits, was Violet's only concession to the changing times.

We had never sat here, although it would have been an ideal place to meet, warm and dry, an escape from the frequent wet spells. It was far enough from where I was staying, yet close enough for it to be a pleasant walk. Some stirring of caution stopped me from bringing him here; I would wait for him at the table and the instant I saw him clear the hedge and stand at the gate to the small compound, I would rush to pay for my tea. I always bought a packet of biscuits for us, a different one each time, which we would share afterwards on that cold damp bench in the park at the bottom of the hill.

The park—our park, I christened it later—was where I had first met him on a dim afternoon. I had been sitting on my bench, one that was by itself and away from the rest, from where I had a view of the pond framed by the willows. Although the park was always full of people, very few found their way to this isolated spot. That afternoon, as he made his way to my bench, I had been surprised and not a little annoyed.

'Good afternoon,' he had called out.

I looked as blank as I could manage and appraised the approaching figure. A young man, in his late twenties, pleasant face. Quite nice eyes, I had to admit, something attractive about the lazy, sleepy, hooded look.

There was nothing good about the afternoon though. It was another gloomy one, punctuated by the occasional drizzle—normal weather for Shillong at this time of the year. My parents had sent me up here to spend time with the Sarmas, old family friends, to take my mind off things. To get away from it all, they said, and I could have laughed. Get away from death and loss, to this dismal weather! Rahul had died and that was that. There was no getting away from it and never would be.

The young man wishing me could not have known any of this and sat down with a further greeting. 'How are you?'

I nodded. How could I be? The doctors said I was not well and I suppose I was not.

'Here, drink it while it is still hot.' Violet placed the cup and saucer gently on the table in front of me and put down a plate of chocolate chip biscuits next to it.

They were his favourite, the chocolate chip ones were. As I dunked one into the tea, softening it, I felt a hard spurt of anger. Where was he? He did not own a mobile phone—too modern for him, he had said and laughed—so I could not call him to find out. He was odd that way about some things. Old-fashioned, he said he was. Always holding my hand to help me across puddles. Making sure he held the gate open for me. Watching from the foot of the hill as I made my slow way up. He made me laugh, sometimes, with his silliness.

I smiled. My anger melted just as quickly as it had appeared. I could never stay angry with him for long. Something in his manner, an utter lack of guile, a certain directness he employed in his dealings with me, disarmed me. I, who had been so wounded and was so suspicious of what the world had in store for me, had been disarmed by this man who had miraculously appeared on my bench.

He spoke to me of so many things people hesitate to speak to each other about. How he felt when it rained and when the sky cleared up and the world was as if washed anew. He spoke of watching his mother cook for him—before she died, she passed away when he was fifteen—in their small kitchen and how loved that had made him feel. 'No one can take your mother's place,' he said and looked away at a white swan gliding on the pond.

He told me how keenly he looked forward to holding his firstborn in his arms. 'I will feel like a king,' he said and laughed. This time it was I who looked away, at a rainbow arcing across the late afternoon sky.

A month after we met, he held my hand in his and said, 'I think I love you.'

Very simply and without hesitation, because it was the right thing to say, I replied, 'I love you too.'

His hands were warm, his skin always dry as if he burned with a fever that was invisible. His palms were rough, there were calluses on the tips of his fingers. 'That is because I am a carpenter,' he said. He worked with his father, whom he had not wanted to leave after his mother's death. 'A long, long time ago it all was,' was how he put it.

We only ever held hands. This was too public a place. He never offered to take me home and I could not bring him to where I lived either. Just once, as evening fell, and the light leached out of the nook we sat in, he had bent his face to mine and kissed me. His lips were dry, as dry as his hands.

When he asked me to go with him for the weekend to Cherrapunjee, I agreed right away. He would borrow his uncle's car and we would stay there in a cottage he'd rent from a friend. I was excited and made devious plans for the outing. Of course, I could not tell the Sarmas, they would never let me go, hence I had packed a small duffel bag, not a suitcase, and snuck out when they took to their bedroom after lunch for their usual afternoon nap. It had already begun to rain and I did the best I could under the flimsy umbrella. By the time I arrived at Violet's shop I was quite wet. Two o'clock, he had said. He would stop at the gate and toot and I was to follow at a discreet interval.

I had sat down at the table at a quarter to two; it was five now.

A loud thunderclap in the sky. The lights went out.

'Don't worry, child,' Violet's voice rang out from the darkness at the back of the shop. 'I will get the lamp.'

The chemical smell of kerosene floated in from where she was and then she appeared, a lamp in her hand. She set it down on my table. After a minute's silence she sat down across from me and reached out for a biscuit.

'What is your name, dear?' she asked.

'Maya,' I said.

She asked what I was doing in Shillong. I told her my son had died three months ago. He had been four last summer and then he went and developed a leukaemia that could not be cured.

'I am so sorry, dear.' Violet reached out across the red checked tablecloth and patted my hand.

'Thank you,' I said. 'I suppose I am here for a change of air.'

'Are you waiting for someone today? Or is it the rain keeping you here?'

I kicked my duffel bag sitting guilty on the scrubbed pine floor deeper under the table.

Then, without any definite reason, I told her about him. I must have wanted to share my extraordinary story with

89

someone, for it all poured out. I told her everything. When I finished, the rain had stopped although the lights were still out.

Violet sighed and straightened up in her chair. 'Well, child,' she said. 'I think I will lock up now. It has been a long day.' She turned around as she got up. 'It must be the rain that has kept him.'

'Yes,' I said, glad that someone else thought so too.

I sipped at my cold tea, happy just to watch Violet as she went about putting things back in their place: jars of jam, shampoo bottles and a box of matches. There was a comfort in the simple ritual of watching hands do good work. I understood how he had felt watching his mother cook.

Violet locked the front door carefully. Rainwater gurgled down the guttering to an invisible cache. A few drops dripped down from the eaves on to her bent head. I waited by the gate for her to finish. She said she lived just below the shop; there was a set of steps at the back of the compound that led down to her house.

'Goodbye, Kong Violet,' I said.

'Bye, love.' She raised her hand and blew me a kiss. 'Wait,' she suddenly said. 'What did you say this young man's name was?'

'John,' I said. 'John.'

Violet cocked her neat head and looked at me. 'Do you mind if I walk a little way with you?' she asked, unexpectedly.

I was surprised but we had both been cooped up all day and I could understand her wanting to stretch her legs.

The winding road was dark; night came early to the hills and the power had not come back on yet. Weak lights flickered in the windows of the houses we passed by, candles and lamps and some lucky house with inverters.

We fell into an easy rhythm. The road sloped upwards and we did not strain ourselves.

'Where did he say he lived?' Violet asked again.

I grew a little annoyed but answered politely. 'At the end of this road, actually. I have never seen his house though. I turn right at the next intersection.'

When we approached the turning, Violet laid a hand on my arm. 'Do you mind if we walk on a little?'

I was growing impatient but continued to humour the old lady. 'Sure, if you want.'

We walked on in silence. The occasional car swept past us, its skin wet and glistening. Once or twice, we crossed men, solitary mostly, and once a pair, clipping down the footpath at great speed, their shoulders hunched against the cold. At the end of the road, Violet stopped. A hedge grew to my right, well over my head, but there was an iron gate set into it.

'Here it is,' she said and pointed beyond the gate. 'John's house. John and Desmond Wallang's house. Father and son, both good men. Carpenters they were both.'

I did not understand. There was a shell of a small cottage where she was pointing, the roof had fallen in, and in the weak light I could see the walls were blackened and crumbling.

'There was a fire, child,' Violet said, her hand on the gate. 'A long time ago, thirty years, maybe more. It was not uncommon, a spark from a fireplace and a wooden house would go up in flames.'

Violet turned around to face me. She put her palm on my cheek. 'John Wallang died in that fire, dear. His father along with him.'

I shivered as a cold wind blew down from the top of the hill. It touched my face as if in greeting and vanished.

CLAWS

Durjoy Datta

Durjoy Datta is the author of twelve bestselling books, including *Of Course I Love You, She Broke Up . . . I Didn't!*, *World's Best Boyfriend* and *You Were My Crush*. Co-founder of Grapevine India Publishers Pvt. Ltd., a mainstream English-language publisher which promotes young talent in the publishing industry, he has to his credit six television shows and over 1000 episodes.

Smriti's husband had been lying to her, and she would have never found out had she not passed that building again. It was a two-storey house, a good ten kilometres from the nearest road. She had complained to Abhishek the first time they had gone there for her check-up. 'Why not any other hospital? Where is it anyway?'

'This is where everyone in the Bose family is born.'

'Here? The affluent Bose princes and princesses born in the middle of nowhere?' she had asked, mocking him as she often did. You can never quite predict the eccentricities of the rich—least of all the Boses. She had been wary of marrying into the Bose family—too wealthy, too guarded, a family bound by virtue of having the same blood coursing through their veins. The daughters and sons, the kids, a family of twenty-five, and they all lived in the same palatial house in Narendrapur—a suffocating, loving family invested in each other's lives more than was necessary. Sometimes Smriti felt like a small odd part in the monolithic, living, breathing organism that the Bose family. It was only during the Durga pujas that the doors of the family house were opened to outsiders. But soon she had gotten used to the lack of privacy, the early-morning *aartis* that lasted an agonizing hour, the saris and the heavy sindoor, the community kitchen and the frequent fasts.

'At least see the nursing home first,' said Abhishek.

She hadn't suspected a thing. Not the fact that there wasn't a moment's hesitation on Abhishek's part as he navigated the broken, deserted roads on the outskirts of 24 Parganas. He told her it had been a decade since he had been there, when his older brother's son was born. Abhishek would have been sixteen at the time and yet his eyes hadn't flitted once during the entire drive.

Her doubts about the hospital had been laid to rest once they entered Ganguly Nursing Home. The doctors were nice, the nurses polite, the floors shining like mirrors, the air filled with a pungent, sterile yet assuring smell—the interior belied the rickety, ramshackle exterior. Three days after that visit, the doctors' reports dealt an ugly blow. Hidden beneath the percentages and the medical terms was a simple truth: she would never be a mother. Her womb was too weak to carry a child to term. She had blamed the nursing home, the contaminated centrifuge, the incompetent pathology lab of the nursing home, the smiling doctor whom she had admired when she had met him. Had it been her sister-in-law Amrita, the demure, quintessential wife and daughter-in-law, she would have quietly accepted her inadequacy, and blamed it on the Bose curse. *Eishob oi petnikaron e* (It's all because of that witch), Amrita and the other Bose women had said when they'd found out about Smriti's condition.

A daughter of two professors, with two decades of education behind her, Smriti considered the mere idea of the Bose curse to be ridiculous. Abhishek had mentioned it to her on what was the first date of their whirlwind romance. Her ears had pricked up when she had heard the word 'curse'.

'Tell me everything!' she had squealed in delight. A nervous Abhishek had then told the story. Hundreds of years ago, the Bose family had been wealthy, tyrannical zamindars who would routinely spear pregnant women workers to terminate their pregnancies and keep them working in the fields. They would carve out their foetuses and bury them in the very land they worked on. And as all curses work, on a stormy night, an especially vengeful woman, bleeding all over herself, summoned all the *petnis*, and cursed the Boses.

'What was the curse?' she had asked, rubbing her hands in inappropriate glee.

'It went something like,' Abhishek had said, 'the Bose family will pay in blood, their legacy soiled and destroyed, the children they killed will rise up from the ground, crawl into the pregnant Bose women and slay their own mothers.'

'Savage. Pretty wily then, the Boses, for making sure their lineage survived. Also, it's kind of strange to date someone from a lineage of child murderers,' she had said and laughed. Abhishek hadn't joined in the laughter. Only later did she discover that Abhishek's mother had died in childbirth. She had put it down to coincidence. After getting married, she had heard the curse being muttered about in hushed tones, and referred to countless times. The supposed curse's effects were now being interpreted in different ways in the extended Bose family—congenital defects, premature deliveries, difficult pregnancies. 'Pregnancies are tough in this family,' she had often heard the women say. When the news of her weak womb broke in the family, they all nodded like it was expected. Educated rationalists being reduced to mumbo jumbo.

All the Bose women came together to tell her that it was okay, that there were options, it was nothing to be sullen about. Like Amrita, she was advised to try out gestational surrogacy. Reading material was swiftly handed over to her, the doctor came home one day and gave her the rundown on what needed to be done. The birth of a child was rapidly reduced from a human experience to an experiment. No one gave her any time to process it all. She had refused the suggestions and had wanted to get a second and a third and a fourth opinion. Abhishek and his brother, Arun, had both resisted at first.

'We don't want you to be disappointed. The doctor you met is the best in the field,' they had echoed.

Yet she had persisted. Abhishek and Arun took her to a few more hospitals, the best in the business, to doctors who were friends. The results were the same and just like the Bose brothers had predicted, disappointment followed. The family seemed adept at handling these situations. They had made peace with their wretched luck or the curse.

'I don't need to have a child,' she had retaliated. Which would have been true had it been five years ago. But things had changed. The visits to the hospital, all her friends who had little kids of their own, had driven her to want one, despite Abhishek's disinterest. Six months later, she had gone to Amrita.

'The child will be your own,' Amrita had said. 'Don't meet the woman who bears your child. If you do you will not be able to live down the sadness of having taken the child from her.'

And so, she had got pregnant, outside her body, on a little slide. She could have sworn she felt it happen. A few days after she had given her eggs to be fertilized, she felt a sharp stab in her stomach. She woke up in cold sweat, blood trickling down her thighs. The next day the doctor gave her the news that the embryo had been planted in the woman who was to carry it to term. His pearly white teeth, his Botoxed smile now grated on her. Smriti had heard about the Couvade syndrome in men where they exhibit the same symptoms as their pregnant partner. She felt it too. The overwhelming nausea, the cold sweat, the feeling of your body being fed to a blender. The nightmares about having given birth to a broken egg, to a ravenous dog, a hungry vulture. It's normal, everyone told her, even as the dreams kept getting more vivid, violent, unspeakable. She would wake up in the middle of the night and want to leave the house, drive around.

'And go where?' Abhishek would ask.

'Anywhere,' she would say. 'I'll know where I want to go when I'm on the road.' All the Bose women would sit around her and engage her to distract her from the overpowering urge to run away. They would oil her hair, paint her feet with *alta*, and tell her stories about how they too had had the same urge during their pregnancies.

In the past eight months, she had often wanted to meet the woman who was going to deliver the child but the Bose women had always stopped her. 'You're not strong enough,' they would chorus.

Until today.

The building where the nursing home had been bore an abandoned look. She hadn't meant to come this way. It was half an hour out of the way but an irrational notion that the woman who was carrying her child would be in the hospital drew her towards it. The doors were locked and it looked like it had been that way for a long time. As she turned away she heard a screeching sound pierce the air. She chose to ignore it and began to walk away when she heard it again. Must be a stuck cat, she thought. She awkwardly climbed the little wall and jumped inside. The thick layer of dust was punctuated by shoeprints that seemed recent. *Someone* was here. Her heart throbbed. She followed the footprints inside—same size, multiple visits. She tiptoed inside. She wanted to leave but found herself incapable of turning back, the rush of adrenaline sweeping away the fear.

The inside of the nursing home was just as she had first seen it. Only dirtier. The stretcher, the beds, the desks and the waiting chairs were covered with white sheets, the tubelights and the fans carefully wrapped in plastic. Like someone intended to return. The doctors' rooms were closed but not locked, the computers and their tables and chairs all covered carefully. She switched on the lights and they flickered to life. Her curiosity had led her to sift through the files in the cabinet when she heard that loud screeching noise again. She turned on her heel and found herself running towards the noise. The closer she got to where she thought the noise was coming from, the greater the overwhelming dread that she was not alone. She wanted to turn back but her instincts said otherwise. Slowly, she pushed open the door. The room was empty. A metal bedpan on the floor. A hospital bed to one side. There was no one. She breathed easy.

She trudged to the end of the room, slapped a chair clean and sat down. And that was when she noticed how clean this room was, unlike the rest of the nursing home.

Back home, she asked Abhishek—as she often did—if the child and the woman were doing fine. He said they were. She asked if the doctor would deliver the child at the same nursing home they'd gone to.

'Of course, Smriti. Where else?'

'Have you seen her any of these days?'

'Only last week at the nursing home. She had some tests to do,' he said.

'I want to be there when it happens.'

Abhishek held her and made her sit down. He told her it would be a traumatic experience for her to see her child being delivered by someone else, that it was better for her to stay home and wait for her child. Smriti's skin crawled under Abhishek's touch. She searched for signs of guilt for lying to her, and found none.

———

Three days later, her deepest suspicions came true. The results of the tests she had taken unbeknownst to the Bose family were here. Smriti could have a child. The previous reports—from three separate hospitals—were false. How could three competent doctors botch up a simple test? There was an easy answer for everything. The doctors had been paid to make her believe she couldn't carry a child to term, a fake hospital had been set up, ready to be set up again if need be, and now she was in the middle of a gestational surrogacy. The why and what of it ricocheted in her head, eating her up. Could the family be so superstitious, so paranoid, so twisted that they wouldn't risk a childbirth?

She figured if she had to get to the bottom of this she had to find someone outside the family, someone who had forsaken loyalties to this warped family. She began to dig for cousins, once and twice removed, people who had sworn off the thick centre of the Bose family tree, the one with the inheritance, the one with all the power. She found only two. The Boses were good at purging people from their family once the umbilical cord was cut. She had heard about a cousin of Arun and Abhishek, Rituparna Bose, who had run away, made a life away from this house. She was the mother of a two-year-old child. They met for coffee after Smriti bombarded her with calls.

'The curse exists. That family is wretched. A bunch of liars and crooks,' said Rituparna, a rational woman, working with an IT firm. From her bag she took out the sonogram and the ultrasound reports of her pregnancy. She pointed at the blotchy images. 'I had a C-section two months before the due date. The pain was unbearable.'

'How did the doctors agree?'

Rituparna evaded the question, excused herself and left. Smriti looked at the sonogram left behind. She couldn't make out anything except a little hand, open, disproportionately bigger than the rest of the body.

Next on the list was Sonali Nandi, the mother of a three-year-old child suffering from intellectual disability. Meeting her was tough; her hatred for the Bose family too conspicuous to hide. Smriti tracked her down, found her alone, and forced her into a conversation.

'You are all monsters!' Sonali had shouted. 'It's because of you that my child is . . .'

Without warning she swung at Smriti and caught her square on the chin. She warned her to stay away from her. Stunned but undaunted, Smriti fished out the name of Sonali's doctor after shadowing her. The doctor refused to talk about Sonali's pregnancy at first but his resolve wavered when Smriti offered to make a healthy donation to his department, and promised her silence.

'She tried to kill her child,' said the doctor. 'The pain and the complications were too much for her to handle.'

'What kind of complications?'

'Usually, foetal movements start between eighteen and twenty weeks, when the child is a little developed. But she started feeling them much earlier. She would come to me crying in pain but the ultrasound told us a different story. The foetus was too small and underdeveloped to cause pain. We thought she was lying,' said the doctor. 'Her parents got tired of her complaints. We gave her placebos saying they were painkillers because we thought she was hallucinating. Nothing worked. She was being admitted three, four times a week for pain we couldn't see a reason for. Her screams would keep the entire hospital awake, inhuman screams.'

Smriti grew impatient and asked the doctor to skip to the end because she was sure he had something to tell her.

'She tried to kill the baby,' said the doctor. 'Twice. She fell down the stairs once. No one suspected anything. The second time her husband caught her beating her stomach with a rolling pin. This was the fourth month.'

'Then?'

'They kept her tied to the bed in the last trimester,' said the doctor.

———————

When she left the hospital, all Smriti could think of was the woman who was carrying her child. Were these just random coincidences? Or maybe there was a genetic strain that passed on from the men of the Bose family. Back home, she locked herself in the study with every Bose family album she could find, and charted out the Bose family tree. She delved deeper into all the babies born in the last decade in the Bose family. She cross-referenced births and women absent from pictures for months at a stretch. The more she dug, the more intricate the web became. Almost every woman who had had a child in the last ten years had gone missing from the pictures for the entire duration of her pregnancy. Except Amrita. She wondered if it was another superstition the Bose family liked to believe in—taking pictures sucks out the souls of unborn babies.

She had been slipping in and out of sleep when something odd in a picture she had glanced at suddenly came into focus. Amrita, as usual, was in a corner of the picture, shying away, but her hands were firmly on her stomach. The sleep in her eyes disappeared. Frantically she arranged a timeline of Amrita's pictures over the period of her marriage. Her appearance hadn't changed much except on two occasions. Her doubts were proven true. She had been pregnant, not once but twice in three years, but neither pregnancy had been carried to term.

Smriti slipped into bed with her husband, snuggled up to him and asked, 'Did Amrita di ever get pregnant?'

He did not meet her eye. 'No, she had the same tests done as you.'

When Smriti confronted Amrita with all that she had gathered, the other woman denied everything. 'I had gained some weight,' came the explanation. 'You're losing your mind,' said Amrita in a tone she had never used before. 'Don't get into things you don't understand.' The same thought was echoed by the Bose brothers when they got back from work. Her requests to meet the surrogate mother were rejected.

'She's resting. And she doesn't want to meet you. It's her request,' snapped Arun.

'I don't care what her request is,' said Smriti. 'I want to see her. Where's she?' She chose to withhold the information about the abandoned nursing home.

It soon devolved into a shouting match where Smriti was called difficult, accused of endangering her own child's future and whatnot. The Bose women ganged up like evil sirens, cried and shouted her into silence. That night, she walked out of the house, promising only to return when her child was born. Abhishek, her loving husband of five years, didn't stop her. Exactly what she wanted. She didn't go to her parents'. Instead, she chose to tail the Bose brothers for the next few days. The first three days yielded nothing. The fourth day she followed them to a government colony in Golf Green. Her husband carried a suitcase chained to his wrist. She followed the brothers up the stairs, to the second-floor house of the man she had seen before—the doctor at the nursing home that didn't exist. They spent half an hour inside, arguing and shouting over something. They left together with the doctor.

Smriti played the distraught wife and had the lock of the house undone by a local key smith. The house was richer from the inside—gigantic LED TV, the latest Mac, a plush leather sofa, and the suitcase lying in a corner. Ironically, the code to the suitcase was her birthday. It was filled with wads of cash. Why were the Bose brothers paying a doctor of dubious credentials so much money? As she rummaged through the drawers, the cupboards, the shelves in the kitchen, a tile under her foot creaked. She shifted the tile to find a bunch of meticulously ordered files in a little rack buried in the floor. She took them all out. Each bunch of files had names of Bose women written in bold over it. Kanika Bose. Chandni Bose. Sharmila Bose. Mina Bose. Sumita Bose. Shruti Bose. Women she had spent five years with.

Frantic, she spread them out on the table. Each file had pictures of women she had never seen before, their medical histories, progress reports of their pregnancies, and on the last page a little stamp: DECEASED.

Before long, Smriti joined the dots. These were the women who had carried the Bose children and had died in the process. That's why there were no pictures of the pregnant Bose women. They hadn't carried their own children and they didn't want the world to know that. Maybe Amrita's failed pregnancies forced them to accept that they had been using surrogate mothers for a long time. But why were so many of them dead? And then she found her file. With trembling fingers, she opened it. Her file had pictures of eleven women, more than all the others, all of them bearing the same stamp on the last page except one. The eleventh one was missing the stamp. She had only begun to grasp what the family was up to when the door opened and the three men walked in.

———

'It's not what you think,' said Abhishek in the loving tone that always worked on her. 'Put down the knife, Smriti.'

'You kill women after they carry these children!' shrieked Smriti. 'But why so many women?'

'We kill no one,' said Arun. 'Now put the knife down.'

A scuffle followed and Smriti didn't see the cricket bat swinging to the back of her neck.

She woke up feeling groggy, her neck pulsing, in a room she faintly recognized. The room she had found in the nursing home. All that had happened came rushing to her. The files. The dead women. Her husband. The Bose women and their children. And the doctor. She got up but stumbled and fell. Her hand was chained to the reinforced-steel door. She looked at the window. The light flickered outside. Four faces stared in—Amrita, Arun, Abhishek and the doctor.

'*Let me go!*' she shouted and that's when she noticed a cannula protruding from her arm.

They had kept her sedated. But now they wanted her to be awake? Why? For how many days had she been here?

'Why am I here?' she screamed.

The faces of the four didn't betray any emotion. Their eyes were stuck elsewhere. Smriti turned to follow their line of vision. Just like her, chained and captive, was a woman on a steel bed. She wore a hospital gown but her swollen belly lay bare. Attached to her were drips and tubes and monitors, all of which beeped urgently.

The woman moaned frantically, her words barely decipherable. Her face as she turned to the side was faintly similar to the one Smriti had seen in her file, only more gaunt and . . . corpse-like. Smriti shouted at the four of them to release the woman. They didn't seem to hear her. Only then did she notice something move inside the woman. A little handprint on the distended stomach, just like in the X-ray.

The woman shrieked. Her screams pierced through Smriti's ears. The four at the window looked on dispassionately. They even smiled a little. The skin pressed outwards, at first one little hand, and then two. A foot.

'What's happening?' asked Smriti.

No one answered; their eyes were glued to the woman's stomach, eager and waiting. The woman's screams were now desperate and wraithlike. The little knuckles pressed harder from the inside, as if the child was trying to tear his way out into the world.

'Do something!'

The screams of the woman became louder. She looked at Smriti. A silent cry for help died in her mouth. And the baby drew first blood. The skin of the woman's stomach broke open, a rivulet of blood streamed down the curvature. Amrita gasped in joy. 'Look, how cute,' Smriti heard her say.

Smriti's throat closed up. The baby's finger now poked out from the little hole in the stomach. The woman raised her head, disbelief washing over the pain. A fist, and then a hand, a bloody little hand protruded, clenching and unclenching. A powerful stench of blood and flesh and evil permeated the air and the tear in the stomach grew bigger and wider. The cry of a demonic child.

'Just a little more, my son,' Smriti heard her husband say.

The crowning. The baby's head pushed through, ripping open the woman's stomach in a big push. Intestines spilt to the floor. The baby's eyes glinted.

'Such a strong boy!' Smriti heard Arun say.

The woman's head flopped about, alive but overcome. Her eyes rolled over. The whites bulged out. And then a loud, clear voice cut through the room.

'The Bose family will pay in blood, their legacy soiled and destroyed, the children they killed will rise up from the ground, crawl into the pregnant Bose woman and slay their own mothers.'

Blood gurgled through her mouth, her body trembled, and ceased to be.

'We have heard that before,' Smriti heard the doctor say.

Smriti wanted to look away but couldn't. Her eyes closed with the woman's.

———

When she woke up, she was back in the Bose house, in her room. She tried to get up but her limbs betrayed her. She figured she must have been sedated again.

'Hey! You're awake,' said Abhishek, rushing to her. He patted her forehead, asking her to rest. 'I know you have a lot of questions. I'm sorry we had to hide all this from you.'

What?

'The Bose family curse is real. It always has been. Our children claw their way out into this world,' he said with a smile. 'For years, we had all the older children conceived by men outside the family. Arun, my own brother, is the son of another man. The Bose legacy was being soiled, our bloodline diluted. All my cousins have the blood of other men flowing through their veins but we are still family. I, on the other hand, am a true Bose. My direct descendants were the only true Boses. My father, and his father, and his father before that, were the youngest sons, sons who always killed their mothers, clawed out of their mother's stomachs. The curse is strongest in us. It's how it works. But then this amazing technology came along. It worked for my cousins, but of course, the curse had weakened over them, and we didn't know if it would work on you. But it did! We lost a few more women but that's collateral. Imagine what you have done for our family! We can have as many children, all completely undiluted. But there's plenty of time to talk about that. It's time to meet your son.'

Abhishek got up, walked to the crib Smriti hadn't noticed before, and brought back with him a little boy. The baby's hands reached out to Smriti.

'And guess what? Amrita is pregnant again.'

THE TIGER LADY OF KABUL

Madhavi S. Mahadevan

Madhavi S. Mahadevan has published two collections of short stories, *Paltan Tales* and *Doppelgänger*. Her most recent work is the novel *The Kaunteyas*.

Ancient cities own their spirits. Kabul, three thousand years old, bears in its dust lost worlds, dismembered lives. Dig anywhere and you will find, in strata after strata, the detritus of past cultures and recent conquests: broken beads, shards of pottery, unexploded bombs, human bones.

I am not an archaeologist or an ethnographer. I have no interest in the past. I am simply a middle-aged policeman serving a tenure of duty in a combat zone. Yet, even I cannot help but feel that the world of spirits, the non-RIP, is too close for comfort. It could be due to the recent bloody history of this country: war-ridden places are said to be haunted by the paranormal. When I first arrived, I heard the stories circulating in expat gatherings—of inexplicable phenomena that soldiers narrated as eyewitness accounts.

'Weird-ass lights,' said one American who had asked to be transferred from a lonely observation post in the hills. 'I saw them through my night-vision goggles.' A Canadian corporal nodded in agreement. He talked of feeling a sudden chill on a warm night, of hearing a man's voice whisper in his ear in a foreign language. *Yeh nyeh panee myoh.* I asked him what the words meant. 'It's Russian for "I don't understand",' he replied. 'The poor sod couldn't figure out what he was doing here—like so many of us.' I laughed. It sounded like a joke.

But the Canadian was dead sober. 'This place is a frigging graveyard,' he said.

A few weeks later the body of a white man was found in an alley. He was identified as a French national employed as a contractor soldier by an international security firm. The previous evening he had been in the company of friends at a private barbecue, but upon receiving a call on his mobile phone he'd left the party suddenly. His throat had been slit. Assassinations of foreigners are not that common any more, since every journalist, aid worker and diplomat undergoes hostile-environment training, while service personnel are put through rigorous risk-sensitization programmes.

Though the Frenchman appeared to have been waylaid, it was clearly not a robbery attempt since his wallet and watch were still on him. His mobile phone, however, was missing. This led the Afghan police to believe that the Taliban was behind the killing. They issued the usual warnings. As the spot where the body was discovered wasn't far from the Indian embassy, where I worked, the police also shared photographs of the crime scene. In the fifth picture I saw a group of Afghan boys standing some distance away in a tightly packed line, staring at the camera. They were bystanders, mostly dressed in loose tunics and baggy salwars, feet shod in open sandals, skullcaps on their heads. A figure at the back of the group caught my eye. He stood in the shadow of an arched entrance to a house. Something about his stance, a stillness, or maybe it was the intensity of his stare, drew my attention.

I called the police officer who had sent me the pictures and, under the pretext of enquiring about the progress of the investigation, asked him if the faces in the picture were known to him.

'Just local youth,' Gul said. 'There's a boys' high school in the neighbourhood.'

'And the tall man in the background?' I prompted. 'The man in a dark overcoat and turban. He's only partially visible because he's standing in a doorway . . . Does he live on that street?'

There was a pause. 'Let me find out,' he said eventually. 'I'll get back to you.'

A fortnight passed. There was a suicide bomb attack at a checkpoint on the outskirts in which a minibus packed with local Afghans caught fire and three men died. It seemed like business as usual in Kabul—except that it wasn't. The NGO money was drying up; the bestselling journalistic accounts had been written; the junior officers' résumés, tacked with a tour of combat duty in an underdeveloped country, had been suitably padded up for the promotion boards back home. Bars were shutting down and restaurants were going up for sale. Afghanistan had served its purpose for conflict entrepreneurs. Like migratory birds, the westerners were leaving.

At a farewell party given by one NGO, I ran into Gul, my police contact. After the usual chit-chat, I reminded him about the tall Afghan in the picture. 'Did you identify him?'

He looked momentarily embarrassed. 'Well . . .' He was clearly reluctant to continue the conversation. 'My subordinate heard something, but it was just gossip, not worth bothering about.'

'All the same I'd like to hear it,' I said.

'They're saying that it was a ghost.'

'A ghost,' I repeated with slow deliberation. 'As in an other-worldly being . . .?'

He said nothing, just looked at me with the faintest hint of a smile.

'Is that what you believe?'

'I'm just repeating the bazaar gossip,' he said evenly. 'Apparently, she is quite well known.'

'She?'

'The Tiger Lady they call her.' Now he grinned, clearly enjoying my surprise. 'She's popular in these parts.'

'You mean she shows up regularly?'

'Not as often now as she did some years ago,' he said. 'The foreigners are leaving, aren't they?'

'What's the connection?'

He shrugged. 'An urban legend, I guess. They say she shows up whenever a white man is killed.'

Someone claimed my attention just then. When I turned back to resume the conversation, Gul was leaving the party. I scurried after him. 'You can't leave me in suspense,' I said. 'I'm a foreigner too.'

He chuckled. '*You* are safe . . . It's the whites she wants out.'

'Is she one of the Taliban?'

'No,' he said. 'She's one of us.'

'What does that mean?'

He gave me a long look. 'She is one of us,' he said again, slowly, with an air of finality.

Over the next day, the strange exchange with Gul kept coming back to me. I studied the picture several times. It was still hard to grasp that the figure in the shadows was a woman.

She . . . *It* . . . was remarkably tall even for an Afghan woman. I estimated her to be at least six feet, or maybe it was just the impression of height one got from that camera angle. The loose edge of the turban covered the lower half of her face, but her eyes were visible. Angry, intent eyes.

Gul didn't seem surprised to get my call. 'Look, I've told you all I know,' he said, clearly exasperated. 'Why don't you just leave the matter alone?'

'An Afghan lady ghost who dresses up as a man and kills white men,' I mocked. 'Come on, Gul.'

'She doesn't kill them,' he said coldly.

'How do you know that?'

There was a long silence.

'If you don't tell me the story, I'll just ask a few questions and get my answers.'

'Take down this number,' he said in a flat voice. 'The man's name is Igor. He was the one who first told me about her. The rest is just gossip.'

Igor—I never learnt his last name—and I met for lunch at a well-known *kababi*. He was a grey-eyed blond with an air of reserve. He had the lean, muscular body and taut skin of a gym addict. He worked for a Russian mining company now, he said, but when he first came to Afghanistan he had been an officer in the Red Army. He called himself an ethnographer, spoke English well, but still retained traces of an accent. I guessed his age to be in the early sixties.

'How can I help you?' he asked.

I had downloaded the picture on my mobile phone. I placed it before him. 'Tell me about her.'

There was no change in his expression, but his eyes widened. He blinked rapidly and looked away towards the sunlit stretch of road where the flow of traffic had come to a standstill: dented cars, dusty trucks, handcarts, buses. After a moment, he turned to look at me. Perspiration beaded his brow. Without looking at the picture again, he reached out and turned the phone face downwards. I removed it from the table and replaced it my pocket. Our food arrived, the waiter served us. 'Tashakhor,' Igor thanked him quietly in Dari. I waited till we had started eating.

'So you *have* heard of the Tiger Lady of Kabul,' I said. 'Have you sighted her?'

To my astonishment, he nodded. 'Once—but it was enough.'

'When did this happen?'

'September 1984. About six months after I arrived in Kabul.'

I leant back in my chair and studied him. Here was a former Russian army officer, a communist, an educated man, by all appearances a rational man, telling me that he had seen a ghost. He read my look and a shroud dropped over his eyes. 'You don't believe me,' he said. 'It's fine. We can talk of something else.'

'No, no,' I protested. 'Being in a war zone, I understand, can be stressful. The mind plays tricks at times.'

'No trick. It was her. In broad daylight.'

He told me then that he had been a member of the Spetsnaz, the Russian Special Forces, recruited from university, where he had been a student of anthropology. His task had been to liaise with the Afghan intelligence service, and build contacts within the intellectual fraternity—journalists and university professors—for profiling the various political factions and tribes in the country, and generating operational intelligence for undercover missions for the Spetsnaz.

'Kabul is the key to Afghanistan,' he said. 'In 1984, when I arrived here, we held it, but over the following months, the mujahideen began to carry out a spate of assassinations targeting us, which ranged from knife attacks in the bazaar to briefcase bombs placed under dinner tables in restaurants. It was around this time that the rumour first surfaced. Naturally, we dismissed it as the irrational superstition of a less developed society. We even thought it was deliberately planted by Pakistani intelligence—they were supporting the mujahideen—to bring down our morale.'

As Igor talked, I was struck by the change in him. He grew more animated. The act of remembering had clearly transported him to another age and a different version of himself: less jaded, more passionate. 'You have to understand,' he said. 'Warfare in the countryside is different. It appears less threatening . . . Here, in Kabul, we held the city, but we were dependent on the Afghan army and police for intelligence. There were betrayals . . . Plenty . . .' He stopped abruptly as a deeper emotion affected him. '*Trust*. It does not spring naturally, but when nurtured it grows . . . The *Pakhtunwali*—you know about it, don't you?'

He was referring to the ancient tribal ethics in Afghanistan that had, for centuries, defined how individuals and communities conducted themselves. *Melmastia*, hospitality, and *nanawatai*, refuge for those who sought it, were an essential part of it.

'I had a colleague who had a lady friend,' he said. 'She was a nurse at the Soviet hospital. He would buy stuff for her—perfume, lingerie, chocolates—from a local smuggler. He had become quite friendly with the man. One day, he got a call, an invitation from this local man . . . It was a trap. My friend's head was found in the middle of a street.'

Reprisal was swift. The street was cordoned off and a house-to-house search conducted. Doors were broken open, women and children rounded up, men thrashed and handcuffed before being taken away by the Afghan police for questioning. 'They had their methods,' Igor said grimly, but did not elaborate on what these were. 'While my men were searching the houses along the main street, I stepped into a narrow side alley with high mud brick walls. There was a door ajar in one wall; through it I glimpsed a courtyard with an old mulberry tree. I remember clearly that there were lines of washing. I pushed the door open. There was no one in the courtyard. I was turning away when I saw a shadow move under the tree. Someone stepped out from behind the trunk. A tall Afghan.'

'A woman?'

'A tall Afghan in an overcoat and a turban. Face partially hidden . . . Exactly as in the picture.' He gave me a half smile, as if he knew how incredible his story sounded. 'It was over thirty years ago.'

I kept my tone non-committal. 'What happened next?'

His face grew pensive. 'I have often wondered about it,' he said. 'I was carrying a Kalashnikov. I could have fired, or moved to drag her outside. But it seemed like a very bad thing to do. I do not know what stopped me from moving forward . . . My friend had been killed and I wanted Afghan blood. But in all that fury, it seemed as though I was face-to-face with something that had even more rage than I did . . . and whose ability to harm me was greater than the protection my rifle could offer.' He stopped abruptly. Maybe he was aware that he sounded a bit crazy. After a minute or so, he spoke again. 'She had a strange stillness about her . . . Have you ever seen a big cat in a forest? That moment when the blend of light and shade takes the form of a tiger. Looking straight at you. There was that sense of . . . of coiled energy. That hard glitter, I will never forget—the burning hatred in her eyes. She . . . she branded my soul.'

He had not fired, nor had he moved towards her. Instead, he had averted his eyes and retreated quietly. He had stood in the quiet lane for several minutes. From the main street, he could hear sounds of women wailing, the shouts of soldiers. The world slowly spun back to being the predictable everyday world he knew.

Igor did not speak to anyone about the incident, not even when rumours of other sightings grew stronger. 'At first, I did not make the connection,' he said. 'Everything was still new to me, and a bit unreal. The official line was to discourage this kind of talk, but another Spetsnaz officer, a phlegmatic man, once spoke of it to me . . . A mysterious Afghan whom he had seen immediately after a Russian journalist was murdered. The Afghan army soldiers were calling it a woman.'

'An Afghan woman, comrade Igor?' I teased.

'A Hindi woman,' he said with a straight face.

I started to smile then realized that he wasn't joking. 'Do you mean a Hindu woman, or a Hindi-speaking woman?'

'I was told that her mother was from Hindustan.'

'Who told you that?'

'Professor Ismail Shah,' he said. 'He would be a very old man now, but if you can you should speak to him. No one knows more about Kabul's history. He may share the story with you.'

The meal ended. I paid the bill. I have to confess that I was beginning to feel suspicious. Was this some kind of practical joke being played on me by Gul and his Russian buddy? And now an Afghan professor? Was the idea that I would make a fool of myself, running around Kabul asking strangers about a lady ghost who may well have been a random Afghan bystander at the Frenchman's murder site? I met Igor's eyes squarely and asked if he had anything else to tell me.

It seemed that he had read my mind about this being a wild goose chase. He said deliberately, without emotion: 'She exists. You may never see her, but she is here. Right here in Kabul. Think about it . . . You have her photograph on your mobile phone . . . Did you Photoshop it? Did someone go to the trouble of staging a picture and send it to you just for the fun of it? The camera does not lie. Whatever the reason for her anger, she is still around. She has been here for a hundred years.'

'What do you mean a *hundred* years?'

'That was what Professor Shah told me. He said that she had been a German agent.'

126

'Two minutes ago you told me that she was from Hindustan.'

Now Igor gave a wide smile. He was clearly enjoying what he considered my ignorance. 'I said *her mother* was from Hindustan. Her father was a German scholar, an anthropologist like myself. He was one of the first Western scholars to study the Kalash people.'

'The Kalash who live in Pakistan?'

Igor nodded. 'Only then it was all Hindustan . . . *British India*.' The emphasis was deliberate, as though he was baiting me. I felt a twinge of irritation. '*You* should understand,' he said. 'In ancient tribal societies, humiliation is never forgotten. A hundred years ago there were people here who were trying to free your country. She was one of them.'

Igor left, but his parting words haunted me. Back in my office I googled the words German spy/Kabul. I got 3,80,000 search results. I learnt something that had not been covered by history texts in school: A hundred years ago, while the world was in the throes of a war of unprecedented scale and destruction (subsequently known as World War I), there was a sideshow going on in this very city, Kabul, that influenced the destiny of India. A German spy mission arrived here as part of a larger diplomatic effort to incite the Muslim world, particularly Persia and Afghanistan, to join a global jihad against the British. Its purpose was to promote rebellion among the Indian Muslims and possibly the Indian army itself. Eventually, the mission failed due to pressure exerted by the British on the Afghan king, as well as the difficulty of supplying and financing a revolt so far from German territory. Among those who developed contact with the German mission were highly influential clerics from India. In a move similar to the one adopted by the Americans to show their support to the Afghans in the 1980s, the Germans published and distributed inflammatory literature citing Koranic verses. These verses enjoined the believers to slay all infidels occupying Muslim lands. Leading this propaganda effort were some of the best Arabists of Austria and Germany.

As I read on, I was drawn into a different world—the world of black-and-white photographs, *solah* topis and khaki, the Union Jack fluttering over the Khyber Pass. It was a world where India was not free, where Indian peasants fought Britain's enemies at the exhortation of recruiters who promised that the empire would reward its loyal subjects with a more representative and just form of government. Was it hope for a future life of dignity that propelled those young men to fight in foreign lands for a cause they knew nothing about? My own great-grandfather had been one of those men: he had fought in Mesopotamia and come home minus an arm. I had never known him, but his sense of anger and betrayal had been handed down like an heirloom. His son, my own grandfather, had joined the Congress party.

That evening, spent reading on the Net, left me with a feeling of gloom. I still had no idea who the mysterious woman was or how she had died, but Igor's words made me wonder if she, too, in some way had belonged to that lost generation— the freedom fighters. Lost because *we* had forgotten their contribution. The German mission had alarmed the British sufficiently for them to impose the law against sedition, the

Rowlatt Act, which in turn had led to the meeting in Jallianwala Bagh in April 1919. In the midst of misery, Hindus, Muslims and Sikhs had united for a common purpose. I recalled a story that my mother had told me about the savage massacre that followed. After the British soldiers had fired their final rounds, an eyewitness said that a dying youth struggled to reach his arm up to the sky and shouted: '*Hindu–Mussalman zindabad.*' I had never quite believed this story, but after reading about the German–Indian jihad, I wondered about it.

I switched off the lights and stepped into the balcony outside my office. The sky was deep indigo, with the scattered glitter of stars, eyes of the universe looking down on the city: the barbed wires, barricades of sandbags, armed patrols.

It took me a while to trace Professor Shah. When I identified myself on the phone, his opening remark to me was, 'I turned ninety-five last week . . . I don't think we should delay this meeting.' Even across the wire, the humour in his voice brought a smile to my face. When I showed up at his house in the old city, his son, an anxious-looking, white-bearded gentleman, led me to his father's library. It was an Aladdin's cave of books. In a luxuriously upholstered chair that seemed almost throne-sized for his shrunken frame sat a wizened old genie: Professor Shah. His face was a parchment map. This was a man who had seen at least eight regime changes in his lifetime and somehow survived. A faint smile appeared on his lips, but his sharp eyes sized me up. I felt very aware that despite his frailty this man would only share as much as he deemed fit.

A servant brought in chai and dry fruits. We began to talk. Professor Shah inquired about my family background and career history. His manner was gentle but pointed, as though he was subtly interrogating me.

'What do you think about the foreign presence in our country?' The question was as loaded as a revolver in a game of Russian roulette. As a foreigner myself, what was I expected to say?

'I believe that every country should have the right to decide its own destiny free from foreign pressure or influence, and should extend the same to other countries . . . Afghanistan has not been allowed to exercise that right.' He nodded as if waiting for me to go on. Wanting to lead him to the topic at hand, I said, 'Your country, for long, was a source of pride for Muslims in India. You defeated the British and preserved your dignity . . . We had to fight and suffer for over a hundred years to make our place in the world.'

'Well, we are fighting now. You suffered in the past. We are suffering now.'

'I hope that those who have fought for Afghanistan will not fade away, as those who fought for India have done.'

The professor's response was unexpectedly quick. 'But *fading away* is what a soldier hopes for. In the fullness of time, a slow erosion of the memory of his sacrifice . . . This is how it should be.'

'Yet there are some whose acts of sacrifice remain unknown.'

A glint appeared in his eyes. 'Maybe she wishes to remain unknown.'

'Then why does she show up when white men are murdered?'

'Not all white men,' he corrected drily. 'Only the British, French and Russians.'

I smiled. 'You mean the Allied powers of World War I,' I said half humorously. 'Isn't that carrying the fight beyond the grave? The world has changed since then.'

'Just a minute ago you were drawing a comparison between India and Afghanistan . . . So how much has it really changed?'

'In those days entire societies would go to war,' I said. 'Today, it's just a handful of people who are prepared to die. Everyone else just carries on with life.'

'And *why* was it different then?' The professor's eyes twinkled.

'Ideology, commitment, a sense of honour . . .' I tapered off. 'Maybe it was that a hundred years ago people were fighting for something bigger than themselves. Today, the world has shrunk and so have we, so have our concerns. Nobody believes . . . not in regular armies anyway.'

'Is that a good thing or bad?'

I thought about it. 'It's good because wars are smaller, but it's bad because societies are fragmented. We do not share the same values any more, so what should we fight to preserve?' I stopped because I realized that I was getting more impassioned than I ought to.

'Go on, go on,' he said as if enjoying himself.

I laughed and shook my head. 'Sir, we'll have this discussion another day. May I ask you about . . . the Tiger Lady?'

'Yes, you may,' he said with a disarming smile. Something in it told me that I had won his approval.

'What was her name?'

'She had many names,' he said. 'No one knew even then what her real name was.'

'Are there any descriptions of her?'

'Yes,' he said but did not elaborate.

'Where did she come from?'

'She was half Indian and half German. Her mother probably came from Nuristan, but it's not known for sure . . . Her father had lived in north India for many years. Not much is known about her early life, where she was born, lived and so on, but we do know that she was educated in Germany. She had a doctorate, one of the first ever for a woman. Although the subject is not known she appears to have been an expert in several languages from this region.'

'What was she doing in Kabul?'

'Her official role was assistant to the head of the German mission, but actually she controlled their propaganda production and distribution.'

I hesitated, then asked the question: 'Why does she always appear as a man?'

He smiled briefly as though recognizing that I was still uncomfortable with the idea of an apparition. 'It is said that she dressed that way because she would accompany German officials to meetings with Deobandi clerics from India. The presence of a woman would have aroused comment so she always kept her face covered.'

'She was just doing her job, yet someone thought that she was dangerous enough for her to be killed . . . Who?'

The lightness disappeared from the professor's face. He studied the floor for a long moment. I took out my mobile phone and placed the picture before him. He stared at it with a strange soft melancholy on his face.

'A hundred years have passed and still she appears,' I said quietly. 'This much anger does not come from a peaceful death or even a sad life. What happened to her?'

'She was betrayed.' He spoke so quietly that I had to strain to catch the words. 'The British had accurately identified her as a crucial link between the Germans and the Indian maulanas who came to Kabul in 1916 . . . The threat of a pan-Islamic jihad was real. One night she was called away by an Afghan who had worked alongside her. A man she trusted implicitly. He lured her to a house on the outskirts of Kabul where three British soldiers killed her. Her body was dismembered and thrown in a ravine.'

'How old was she?'

'Around thirty.'

'What happened to the killers?'

'At least two of them returned to England and lived to a ripe old age,' Professor Shah said. 'About the third, I'm not sure . . . Maybe he too died in his bed.'

I nodded. 'Sir, you have told me an interesting and tragic story, but . . .'

'You don't believe me,' he finished the sentence. 'You need proof, documentation. I have nothing but an excerpt that I copied a long time ago—from a diary. It was among the papers of a British professor who was teaching in Kabul in the 1960s.'

'Was he too murdered?'

'He died in his bed.'

'Was it his diary?'

'I didn't say that . . . It was found among his notebooks and papers. How it got there, no one knows. It was a most ordinary diary, the kind Englishmen frequently kept. I leafed through it. There was nothing revelatory in it, but there was a mention of a murder . . . I copied it down.'

He reached out to the side table and handed me a typewritten sheet.

A most unpleasant business has unfolded here, and I'm afraid of a frightful stink were the competition-wallas in Delhi or London to find out. B learnt that a member of Stoerger's staff in the German mission was the liaison officer of the mullahs. There was a strong suspicion that it was a woman disguised as a man. One cannot fathom why B decided to take the extreme step. To my mind he was irresponsible. It may be that he has lived too long in the wild frontiers where human life means little, especially the life of a woman . . .

Without informing anyone beforehand, he either bribed or threatened one of her Afghan subordinates to call her away ostensibly to render assistance to a sick child. The poor woman trusted the man and went in the dead of night to a house where B and two sergeants were waiting for her. When B later recounted the sordid

incident to me, it was with a disturbing
sense of pride. 'She was a hellcat,' he
said. As instructed, the Afghan ushered
her into a room and bolted the door from
outside. Inside, silhouetted by the
flickering light of a single candle, stood
the men who would murder her, each armed
with a butcher's knife. What did she feel
then? Did she cry out for help or mercy?
B said that it was neither. 'She fought
all the way. By God! Was she strong!' At
one point it even seemed that she would
wrestle a dagger away from her assailants.
Eventually, however, multiple stabs to her
arms and chest weakened her, whereupon the
two sergeants seized her while B pushed
her head back, fully exposing her throat
to his blade . . . Even now when I think
of the monstrosity of this act my blood
freezes. B told me that she was a tigress.
He said that she fought so hard that later
he even felt a bit sad that he had to
kill her. When they lit an oil lamp and
examined her corpse they saw for the first
time what she looked like. B's very words
were, 'She was incredibly beautiful. I
will never forget that look in her dead
eyes . . . There was still a luminosity in
them.' Then his face grew dark with anger
and he said, 'She should have stayed back

in Germany and married a Hun.' He said
that they disposed of her body in a ravine
outside Kabul.

I put the sheet of paper down on the table. For a long time,
I could not bring myself to speak. The professor watched me
silently. Dark, calm Afghan eyes.

'Why was it necessary to kill her?'

'It was not,' he said, his voice vibrating with emotion. 'The
British were already exerting pressure and, as we know, the
king disbanded the German mission. If her murderers had just
waited . . .'

'Did *nobody* look for her?'

'I don't know the answer to that,' he said heavily. 'We only
know . . . that she existed . . . and that her killing was not just
an act of betrayal, but also of unnecessary cruelty. *Afghanistan
was not at war when she was killed.* It was—it was a dastardly
crime. Committed by cowards.'

'And so she still seeks justice.' I looked at him. 'Do you
believe that?'

The professor did not reply immediately. 'I have often
thought about her,' he said. 'Why does she come back again
and again? I have a theory . . . Her murder was a horrible crime.
There may be no connection, but within years of it, everything
fell apart. Our kings were assassinated or overthrown, our
country became a playground for foreign occupiers, our people
became victims of countless murders . . . She was first sighted
during the Third Afghan War. Since then she has appeared
many times. Invariably when a betrayal is followed by a

murder. *Always* when the victim is a white man, a foreigner. The perpetrators have never been caught. There will be no justice for the dead men—just as there was none for her.' He stopped, then spoke again, slowly, 'At the very end of my life, it seems to me that there is a lesson here. Maybe those who wish to exercise the powers of life and death should understand that the consequences never go away.'

Dusk had crept into the room. From a mosque nearby the call of a muezzin floated on the cool air.

'There is a Pashtun saying,' the professor said. '*I took my revenge after a hundred years. And I regret only that I acted in haste.*'

ELIXIR

Usha K.R.

Usha K.R. is the author of the novels *Sojourn*, *The Chosen*, *A Girl and a River* and *Monkey-Man*. Her novels have been listed for several awards, including the Commonwealth Writers' Prize, the Man Asian Literary Prize and the DSC Prize for South Asian Literature. *A Girl and a River* won the Vodafone Crossword Award, 2007. *Monkey-Man* was shortlisted for the DSC Prize for South Asian Literature 2012.

On this street, she thought, must live the whole of humanity. Immediately she realized how tired she was, how very tired.

'Perumal Koil Street,' she had told the cyclerickshaw man at the railway station. He had looked doubtful. She brought out her diary with the address written down and even before he shrugged she realized how useless that was; it was in English, of course. But he hauled her bags in anyway, and set off. There must be only one street where visitors went.

Perumal Koil Street. At the end of the street stood the temple to which she must go. Meanwhile, men, machines and animals jostled for space in the heart of the street. Cement blocks, closely packed, not a hair's breadth between them, thrust on to the street, bellowing, pushing the other out of the way. The storefronts glittered. Every building seemed to house a silk sari shop or a bank. This was an ancient port town famous for its silk weavers and merchants. Now, the sea had receded and the town was inland by miles, and more and more silk looms were turning idle. There seemed to be people living in the upper storeys of the buildings—she could see figures silhouetted against the grills of the small windows and clothes hung out to dry in the balconies. The pavements were occupied by the flower and fruit vendors, who spilt on to the street, unmindful of the traffic, especially the buses, and the people.

The air, even so late in the day, was humid and warm—it turned to acid in her throat. There was no sign of winter though they were well into November. A whiff of the flowers came her way as the cyclerickshaw passed them, piled in heaps for the devout to purchase when they went to the temple for the last darshan of the day. It was turning dark and soon the Lord would turn in to rest for the night.

They stopped at a chunk of cement with a narrow opening on its side. On the ground floor was the shuttered office of V.L. Cooperative Bank. Next to the name board of the bank, barely noticeable, was a small rusting metal board with the name of the lodge. She walked down the narrow passage and entered through a side door. The man behind the counter looked up and looked her full in the face. And this, despite her efforts to blend in.

'I am . . . I'm from . . .' she fumbled. His eyes did not leave her face.

'Kalimurthy—' It sounded like a secret code.

'Ah.' The man looked away from her, satisfied, and would never look her in the eye again as long as she stayed there.

A very young boy appeared to show her the way to her room. He ran his hands over her soft colour-coordinated bags in a quick caress before hefting them on to his head. She followed him up the narrow stairs, waited as he put the bags down and unlocked the room. The boy handed her the padlock and the key—large, heavy and reassuring. There was no question of giving him a tip.

It was a small room with a bed in one corner, a metal table and chair against the wall, and a wooden chest of drawers—needless to say, she had never stayed in a room like this before. The thick rough grain of the bed and the chest of drawers suggested jungle wood, and insects. There was a dented steel jug and steel tumbler on the table. A door from the room led to a small balcony; she was never going to open that door, she knew. The bedsheet and the pillowcase bore the fresh impress of the previous occupant.

But it was a simple place, with uncomplicated arrangements. There was a single light in the room with a single switch, the fan turned at one speed, the bathroom had a tin bucket and mug with a lone tap dispensing cold water, and the doors had old-fashioned tower bolts that fell securely into place.

She sat on the bed and waited. As she watched, a small cockroach made its way along the wall and darted across the floor, and her eye lost it in the pattern of the mosaic floor tiles. There was a time when the sight of a cockroach would have sent her into a frenzy. But now, she was watchful of other visitors; she would sit up through the night and wait for them.

When she woke up in the morning, the room was foggy with the grey dawn light. She bathed in cold water that trickled from the tap into the tin bucket, and made a dash for the temple. She stood for a moment at the imposing gateway to calm herself. There was a row of people sitting outside the gateway, hands outstretched for alms. One of them pointed to her feet. She had forgotten about her shoes! She took them off at the footwear stand, thinking how vicious the spike of her heel looked amidst the worn, flat heaps, and then proceeded to tiptoe across the wet, muddy flagstones into the courtyard.

'Kalimurthy—' Again the magic word.

They were gathered at one side of the courtyard, under the pipal tree, all those who had uttered his name, waiting for the man himself. He will come to you, she had been told, he will decide whose turn it is. All you have to do is wait—you don't have to say anything to him. He will just look at your face, maybe feel your pulse, and he will know. And he was available only in the courtyard of the Perumal temple in the small south Indian town where he lived.

As they waited on the stone platform round the pipal tree, a stream of devotees went in and out of the temple. In the abstract, she loved the idea of the temple, its lofty structure, the symmetry of the pillared halls, the carved pillars and ceilings. She could even visit one on a quiet day. But in the concrete, she found it all excessive: the crowds, the crush of human bodies, the intense smell of incense and flowers, the grit under your toes. She was hesitant to touch the vermilion to her forehead, or take to her lips the *tirtha* that the priest distributed—the fragrant, consecrated water of life. The oil lamp she had always thought messy, impossible to clean. And the image of a lamp flickering in the darkness she had found melancholy, as if it was meant to underline the sadness of life.

———

She was sitting in the glass-fronted lounge bar on the twenty-fourth floor of the hotel. The Mediterranean stretched out at her feet, a choppy, organic, permeable mass, the colour of blue sapphires. The lights on shore glinted like jewels in the night. She had ordered a seafood platter and the man at the bar had suggested a local wine to go with it. The limestone hills of the region and the dry climate made for the perfect terroir for the grapes, he said. She liked the name, Elixir—it seemed to fit her mood exactly—and ordered a bottle.

She swirled the golden liquid in her glass and watched its viscous legs travel down the sides; she stuck her nose in, and breathed to deep satisfaction. When she had started on her corporate career, so many moons ago it now seemed, she had enrolled in a wine appreciation course, which seemed the right thing to do. It had included a tasting tour in a vineyard and from that moment she had been hooked.

She sat back, closed her eyes, and savoured the full-bodied promise of the Chardonnay and Viognier, the fragrance of grass and flowers, the suggestion of vanilla and pears that the wine made good. This was a perfect evening, she thought, a fitting conclusion to the trip. Her company had been in the process of setting up a new unit in partnership with a local group, and she had been sent to complete the last of the processes, to see that the due diligence was done and that the compliances were in place. Her meetings had gone well and she had prepared the way for her bosses to sign on the dotted line.

She recalled her initial business trips abroad, the first few times she had been sent on her own. She would be nervous throughout. The butterflies would flutter non-stop in her stomach and even as she acquitted herself well—extremely well in fact, if not she would not have been where she was just having turned forty—she would be waiting to go home. At the end of the day, when she returned to her room in the hotel, she would slip under the covers and turn on the TV, and at best order something extravagant from room service. Everything seemed to overawe her and she was easily impressed. The items of personal care in the bathroom, for instance, with their unfamiliar textures and fragrances and the fancy bottles they came in, fascinated her. Once, she had taken back three small bottles of a sea-green liquid as a keepsake simply because it was labelled 'Lait Corporel' instead of body lotion. Now, she swept all those aside and set up her own shop of personal-care products, for she was becoming discerning, more particular as she grew older. And the first thing she now did was to check out the swimming pool and the sauna to relax and reinvigorate herself at the end of a business day, and find out about the local restaurants she could sample. Of course, it had called for a lot of . . . well, she wouldn't say sacrifices, but adjustments on her part, some changes in mindset.

When she returned to her room from the lounge after her perfect evening, a draught of air from the windows made the curtains flap—it stopped her dead in her tracks even as she tried to figure out what was odd about it. It must have been from the window because it was certainly not from the air conditioner. The heavy curtains were drawn, but the light gauzy white ones were pulled across the wall-to-wall sheath of clear protective glass. Beyond the balcony and far below, the city lights glowed like warm coals, and the Mediterranean pulsed beyond. She had checked the door leading to the balcony before leaving her room, as she always did, and she pushed the curtains aside to check once again. The lock was still securely in place. The room with its soft light, and her standing in the middle looking uncertain, was reflected in the mirror. She caught sight of herself, and pulled herself together. There was nothing else to do but change and turn in for the night. She had finished calling home and speaking to her mother and her husband, and they were both looking forward to seeing her.

But again, just before she turned off her bedside light, she looked round the room quickly, under the bed and in the closet. Too much Elixir—she shrugged off the feeling. She should not have had a whole bottle of it when she had an early-morning flight to catch.

She mentioned it casually to a friend, immediately after she got home. They were sitting in a lounge bar called the Noon Wine, on a Sunday afternoon, and she was describing the view of the Mediterranean from the window of her room to the friend who rarely travelled.

'I could feel it, that presence, that . . . thing . . . sitting in the chair, looking at me.'

'It must be your alter ego,' the friend said.

She was hurt by that. She felt it was a catty remark, even if it was a joke. But the friend made up after that. She sent her a bottle of rose water to bathe her eyes, to cool them down.

The next time it happened, she was brushing her teeth before going to bed at night, peering into the mirror to look for blackheads on her nose. She was alone in the flat as her husband was travelling on work. Again, a brief, cold blast of air, and her senses were on red alert. Brandy and hot water, she thought, that should fix her nerves. Good thing she had picked up the Rémy Martin from the duty-free shop on her way in.

A few nights later, she sensed it squatting next to the washbasin, its silhouette reflected for a fraction of a second in the mirror—a small face in profile, the curve of a plump cheek, a little nose, but thankfully no eyes, she could not have borne that.

She remembered feeling then as if she had been struck to the core with a heavy object, a physical feeling, a failing of the limbs, a collapse of the shoulders, a feeling of complete defeat. No, she had not been afraid of the . . . the thing, but of the fact that she had sensed it, and seen it. Right then she knew there was no escape from it.

One evening, when she came out of the bathroom, she could tell that the apparition had exited the mirror and entered her room and was sitting on the chair. Of course there was nothing there, only the plump cushion with its mirror-work cover, but she knew. When she switched off her bedside lamp, she heard a sigh, a soft sigh, more like a yawn, and she sensed a small body stretching, a smooth movement of muscles and tendons, like a cat. So she kept the night light on, the zero-watt bulb fitted along the side of the wall, which she had not required so far.

Usually, when her husband was away, her friend came over. They watched a late-night film or went out for a drink, long into the night, and talked till it was almost dawn. When her friend called she said, 'Sorry, not this time. I have a visitor.'

'I'm fine,' she told her friend from the Pilates class. 'I'm just taking some time off.' There was no point, she had decided, just hanging out and talking, and drinking, and doing something just for the sake of it. She needed some time for herself too.

She took a day off and went on a long drive, going no place in particular. She went to the library and revived her membership; so long since she had borrowed a book or a CD. The librarian looked at her pile of books and CDs.

'101 Dalmatians, that's a nice one. I didn't know you had . . .' she began, and caught her eye and broke off. 'Three weeks,' she said. 'You have to return them in three weeks.'

One day, as she was watching a cartoon show just before going to bed, she heard a sound from that part of the room, a kind of loud purring, which she interpreted as a stomach growl, so she went to the fridge and poured herself a glass of milk. It tasted good, which was surprising, because she hated the taste of milk. What was more, it disagreed with her and usually curdled in her stomach. She allowed herself a moment of self-congratulation, on having recognized the sign correctly. Late another night, after she had finished watching a film on TV, a romance which ended in a parting of the lovers, there was an ache in her temples, and her face—dry to the touch—was wet with tears. She must watch out, she thought, be mindful of what her body was trying to tell her.

The creature was shy, she could tell. As soon as her husband returned, it didn't show up for some time. She felt forlorn, as if she had lost a friend. But she knew her husband wouldn't like it if she suggested that he shift to the guest room.

'You are looking different,' her husband said one day. 'What's with these floral blouses, I haven't seen you in these before . . . And your hair?'

She hadn't said anything to him as yet. She had to think carefully about how she would phrase it. He wasn't exactly a fair-weather husband, but his notion of foul weather was zero visibility, nothing less. She would have liked to confide in her mother but she knew that it was a sore point between them. They had had many fights about it before.

––––––––––––––

The GP, their family doctor, said it must be the stress, the pressure of deadlines. She worked too hard. He advised rest, vitamin supplements and exercise in the outdoors, not the gym.

There had been no sign of the . . . the creature for days now, though she had been turning in earlier and earlier each day, staying up half the night, and waking up late . . . And then there it was, in broad daylight, sitting in her clothes cupboard, at the edge of the conference table when she was making a presentation, making her mix up her slides, and once even on the pavement, threatening to step off into the thick of traffic, causing her to shriek, and for people to turn their heads and look at her.

'I think you should take a taxi to work and back,' her husband told her when he noticed the high seat in the back of her car. As if it was any of his business! 'Driving may be too much of a strain.'

The ophthalmologist shone a bright light into her eyes and made her read letters off a chart on the wall. What kind of image did she see? Was it static or moving? When did she see it? How frequently? Was it real or imaginary? The flecks that floated in her eyes when she closed them, were they black or white or translucent?

'I don't know,' she said. 'Perhaps. Maybe. Sometimes.'

The doctor rubbed his eyes. He looked tired and in need of a doctor himself.

Had she had a fall? Had she hurt herself? He tapped the back of her head with his pen. 'Let's rule out a tumour in the occipital lobe.'

She came through her retinoscopy and her MRI scan with flying colours.

Her office recommended that she take the long-deferred sabbatical, which they had earlier refused, saying they could not afford to part with her for such a length of time at so crucial a juncture in their plans.

'Don't worry, we'll get through this together,' her husband said, taking her hands in his.

'Get through what? And what do you mean together?'

Her mother called. She wanted her to meet a priest to whom she had sent her horoscope. 'Your horoscope and your husband's,' her mother said. 'He has a reading for you. Will you go and see him?'

She hadn't the energy to argue with her mother. So she said yes.

It was much like a doctor's waiting room—all of them sat on plastic chairs in the annex attached to the temple outside a room that said 'Office', with the same inward-looking, slightly anxious expression. The priest came late, riding in on his scooter, in civvies, and went in to change, emerging in his garb, much like a doctor in a white coat. He was a handsome man, the priest, young, his hair in a crew cut, wearing a white dhoti with a gold-edged *angavastra* thrown round his shoulders. He had a deep chest and rounded shoulders. He wore a necklace of *rudraksha* beads and stripes of holy ash flaked freshly off his chest hair. The computer-generated and tabulated document that he laid out on the table could well be a medical report, only a few details and fields being different. Instead of the haemoglobin count and the urine analysis, there were planets and constellations and signs of the zodiac, telling details all the same about your health and state of mind. He laid the document out on the table and with the brisk air of a professional, a service provider, he explained the mismatch in the squares, the misalignment of the stars that had arisen, that could be causing 'the problem'. He would arrange for a shanti *homa* to be performed. He reached for a drawer in the table and wrote out a receipt.

She had a roaring fight with her husband. 'Why have you asked my mother to come and stay with us? You don't even like her . . .'

Her husband dusted the bed and shook the crumbs on to the floor. He pulled Joey from under her pillow and threw him into the balcony. 'Hey,' she said, 'hey,' and ran to retrieve him.

'Stuffed toys? For heaven's sake!'

She could see he was under a lot of stress. There were dark circles under his eyes.

'I beg your pardon,' she sang to him, an old-time song that she remembered, 'I never promised you a rose garden . . .' She used to do that a lot in the old days, when they were newly married, sing snatches of songs to him.

'Stop that,' he said. 'Please.'

'Is there a rule that you have to be the same all your life? Look the same, behave the same, have the same friends? All your life?' she said.

He sat down on the bed and covered his face with his hands. 'Have you looked at yourself in the mirror?' he said. 'Do you see how you look? When was the last time you visited the parlour? I've never seen your nails like that, chewed to the quick . . . And the food? I find pizza delivery boxes everywhere. And you are on the verge of losing your job . . .'

How fragile he was. How quickly he was going under. She must be kind to him. She would take no notice that he was calling her a fat, greedy, slovenly slob.

'I am not losing my job,' she said mildly. 'I am on a sabbatical.'

He lay back heavily on the bed, not looking to see if it was her side of the bed or his, and flung his arm across his eyes. 'The doctor, the other one whom the ophthalmologist recommended, has asked that your family be here. That is why I invited your mother to stay.'

———

How much he spoke, the other doctor, also a man—too many men around—asking her questions, probing, probing, probing into things that weren't his business, or anybody else's for that matter, with her husband and her mother sitting on either side. She felt as if she were back in school again, summoned to the princy's office.

She spoke and she spoke and she spoke. He listened with alert, intelligent eyes, like an animal on the hunt. At the end of her assigned hour, he capped his pen and closed his black book. She talked about her schooldays. Yes, she had never been second at anything all her life, at school, at college, at her job. Everyone said she took after her father, who had died early. Yes, she was the best at her job, only of late she was not, not being distracted but thinking of things a little differently. Her perspective had changed, that was all.

Her mother wept. She brought up long forgotten things; her younger daughter, born much after the first one, who wasn't quite all there and who did not live long. Her husband— she suspected he only wanted an excuse to talk—brought up completely irrelevant anecdotes, and then suddenly mentioned his hernia, inguinal hernia he called it, and the surgery and, well, its aftermath. That was the time they knew they had taken the right decision about having children.

'You know,' the hunter-doctor spoke at last, sounding apologetic, 'human beings are the most complicated creatures on earth. We never know from what deep fountain our wishes arise and how they are fulfilled.'

She settled down. She took the pills that he prescribed and set up weekly appointments, and then monthly. She spoke some more. Finally he said she need not come to see him any more. It was the doctor's receptionist who gave her the contact, pressing a slip of paper with a name and a telephone number into her hand as she went past her desk after her last session. It was one thing to find a cure, she said, and another to be healed.

———

She was settling down quite nicely in her room. It wasn't so bad once you got used to it. She now had a routine of sorts, had found a regular fruit-seller and flower-woman. She chatted with them sometimes. And also with Thambi, the boy at the lodge who brought hot water up in a bucket every morning and ran errands for her. She shopped for fresh sheets and pillowcases from the market—they were not bad for the kind of place this was. She opened the balcony door in her room, and now hung her washing on the lines there. As for her nightly visitors, the cockroaches, she had dealt with them. She had discovered a wonderful thing called Lakshman Rekha, literally The Line That Must Not Be Crossed—it was a piece of chalk, like a child's crayon, and all she had to do was draw lines with it along the wall and the tap in the bathroom, and that put an end to them. For a moment she felt a pang for these creatures, so old, older than the dinosaurs, such doughty survivors, that now lay still, legs up in the air, felled by a chemical that had altered their states completely.

In the evenings, every evening, she called her husband and her mother from the booth downstairs, and spoke to them. They seemed to be getting on better with each other (and with her!) now that she was away. Yes, she was not forgetting to take her medication, she assured them. She sent messages for her colleagues. She would be back soon. Sometimes, Mr Prakasam, her 'minder', appointed by her husband, visited; thankfully, he was quite discreet.

Her turn was yet to come. In the morning, after her bath, she made her way to the temple. She had bought herself a pair of flip-flops—the basic kind, white with blue rubber straps—to wear on the streets. He had still to send for her. He caught her eye and smiled, they had come that far. She had to say that she had developed some kind of kinship with the group that waited every morning for Kalimurthy. She recognized a couple of others as her fellow lodgers—a middle-aged married couple, and a young woman accompanied by an older male guardian—and they smiled a tight smile when they saw each other, and that was all, no more. There was a boy in a wheelchair whose mother fed him with *ganji* and wiped his mouth carefully after each spoonful—she spent the whole morning feeding him and wiping his mouth. An elderly woman, dressed in a skirt and blouse, a girl's clothes, wandered in the courtyard and round the temple, singing to herself.

It was surprising how ordinary Kalimurthy looked—you would not notice him in a crowd. According to Thambi, he used to be an insurance agent and had now retired. He just stepped in every morning, without fuss, and sat on the stone seat next to the platform round the pipal tree. From his cloth bag he took out an exercise notebook and jotted some things down. He had all their names—anyone new had their name entered into that notebook. Then he would go and sit next to one of them in the group or call them up to his seat, and to the others it looked like he was chatting with them, as if with a friend, or an acquaintance, or even a stranger whom one asked for directions or the time. Sometimes he would hold the other person's wrist, or chant a prayer, asking them to repeat after him, or slip them a piece of paper with instructions. One day he paused by the wheelchair and gave the boy an orange. She had heard that he often recommended a course of treatment or a doctor to consult. But he was a healer in the true sense of the term, according to her. One who sensed your need without any questions, with no intrusive examinations, and provided answers as unobtrusively. Sometimes, people said, you were already cured and you didn't even know it.

———

She buys lengths of sevanthi and jasmine flowers from the flower-woman and sweet limes from the fruit-seller that morning. The flower garlands she drapes round the trunk of the pipal tree and the fruits she offers to Kalimurthy as a mark of respect. He takes them from her with a smile, makes eye contact, and puts them into his bag. Sometimes he gives the fruits to someone else. A few times he has touched them in blessing and given them back to her.

The flower-woman has her daughter with her that morning, a girl of about seven or eight, in school uniform, with very dark eyes and a serious face, almost melancholy.

'My little girl used to be exactly like this,' she tells the flower-woman. The woman smiles and says nothing.

The fruit-seller has managed to get hold of apples and has a pile of them. She shakes her head—she has a lot of fruit already. She eats so little these days; one meal in the middle of the day and fruits at night. But she must have her coffee in the morning, just like her father. She is reminded more and more of him these days. Thambi brings her coffee in a flask first thing in the morning. She thinks of her father who would inhale deeply the steam curling out of his steel tumbler of filter coffee, take a sip, sit back and say, the gods may have their nectar, their tot of immortality. I know what it is for me. For me, it is this that makes life worth living.

THE FACE

Manabendra Bandyopadhyay

Manabendra Bandyopadhyay was born in 1938. His first teaching job was in Myanmar, after which he taught comparative literature at Jadavpur University, Kolkata, till 2002. He has written 70 books, including translations of his work into Hindi, Urdu and English. His work is much awarded, including by the Sahitya Akademi.

A long, long time will pass thereafter. Finally Sita will waste away into nothingness one day. And will anyone remember afterwards that the morning dew had glistened under the rays of the sun here once upon a time? Only the solitary rosewood tree may retain the memory of the dew for a few weeks. Then, when winter comes, it will shed its leaves, overcome with sadness as it gazes at the tender glow of the declining sun. After that, one morning, it will surprise itself under the red sun—because it has been coloured by fresh leaves. It will not even remember this moment of its solitude.

The afternoon sunlight lay on the other side of the glass window. It had created a square patch of light on the marble floor this side.

Sita rose from her soft, milky-white bed. She opened the window with her sick, pale colourless hand. A perfect late afternoon tumbled on to the marble floor. Sita stood at the window, holding the bars. The lawn with its flowerbeds and gravel path lay beneath. A row of wild casuarinas, clumps of tall almond trees, patterns in green on the leaves of mango trees, golden frangipanis like the tender long fingers of a princess. There was the porch, and the gate at the other end of the lawn.

Oh, how long it had been since Sita had been out. After aeons she had walked as far as the gate the other day. She had even been about to give some instructions to the gardener, but she couldn't continue when the face floated up before her eyes with unbearable clarity. She had returned, ashen with fear. Walking across the veranda with the marble floor, she had entered this room on the second storey. Then she had slumped on her foamy white bed, sobbing into her pillow for hours.

What else could she have done?

New books from the library arrived in the post almost every day. Books wrapped in shiny new cellophane resembling glass. Expensive books. How much people could write! Sita no longer enjoyed reading. She found it tedious. Even the newspapers seemed insipid. For how long could you just brood silently? Her senses reeled, fat teardrops rolled down her bony cheeks, and when they reached her lips, what else could she do but bury her face in her pillow?

How lonely it was in this huge house!

Sita took her hands off the window bars, tearing her eyes away from the sky. She glanced at the walls. At the walls and at the clock. It was late afternoon. She glanced at Saroj's oil painting. A handsome Saroj, bursting with health. She glanced at the table. The vase held a bunch of rajanigandhas. Sita had no idea when the gardener had changed the flowers. Perhaps she had been asleep. The white tablecloth had a lovely pattern on it. White lace. Embroidered by Sita.

She walked up to the table, running her pale thin hand over the pattern.

What would Sita do now? The room was getting dimmer in the darkness. Evening was descending on this tiny room on the second floor.

Sita switched on the light. The room glittered brightly as soon as she pressed the switch. Maybe Sita's life could have glittered the same way.

She opened a drawer. A square box filled with blue notepaper lay within. Letters. She withdrew one of them lightly. Not only had the ink not faded, there was even a faint, sweet fragrance on the paper. Then why had everything ended for Sita? Why had it all ended for her?

Bikash had sent the letters to Sita on her wedding night, adding a comment in a sharp, distinct hand. 'What do I need these letters for any more? You can keep your own letters.'

Sita's gaunt face paled further at the thought of her wedding night. She picked up another sheet of blue notepaper from the box. She reread the much-read letter, written in her own hand, one more time.

As I sit down to write after a long, long time, I wonder why I cannot become any less ardent even after everything's been said. Where will the priest find flowers every morning? And yet he cannot pray without flowers. Don't laugh. I'm the one in trouble. I want to tell you something, something that can present my thoughts properly, beautifully, but everything goes haywire.

So many thoughts. If you could read my mind, you'd be astonished.

I miss you so badly.

When bathing in the sea, sometimes I get out of the water to lie on the sand. Alone, all alone. Resting my head on my hands, I look at the foam on waves. Small flecks of white foam, just like your smile. The early-morning light makes patterns on my face. The sunshine fringes the quivering feathers on the seagulls' wings. I am reminded of you. It feels as though I only have to turn sideways to see you smiling at me. Or as though you're going to take my hand any moment and pull me into the water.

I return, splashing water from my wet sari after bathing. Sand falls from my hair. I take the trail by the casuarinas. It feels as though you're walking by my side. I don't want to look around. If I do, I'll discover you aren't really there. That's not what I want. You're there. You're there by my side, in the blue of the sky, in the wind, everywhere, in my heart. I don't want the road to end, ever.

But how can it not? The gate to the house is just a short distance away. Nor are you by my side. Once inside, I let myself go under the shower. And then the monotonous day follows. It's horrible.

Really, Bikash, believe me. The rain rang out like the sound of anklets the other evening. I began to miss you so very much as I looked at the dim shape of the casuarina grove. I seemed to be able to smell your cigarette clearly. I could feel the heat from your body, your amused glance.

The one thought that keeps coming back to me these days is that there are no turnings in life. I feel so helpless, so angry, at times. I wonder whether I'll ever have a space only for myself, for my soul.

Maybe this will surprise you. You might even smile slyly when you hear this story. The story is a glaring example though of how I've become obsessed with you. The fish was cooked in a new way for lunch yesterday, with a new gravy. It was excellent. I loved it. So I thought I'd learn the recipe. The very next moment, I remembered you saying that you don't care for gravy very much. What was the use of learning it then? Nothing could inspire me after that. I couldn't bring myself to pick it up.

I'm sure it's a very amusing story, but can you imagine my plight? Even things I like are irrelevant to me unless they're after your heart.

It may not be a bad idea to make a resolution not to accept everything you say. The way things are going, maybe you'll be bored too by such a faithful Sita. I suspect both of us have forgotten how to quarrel. I wonder how people can waste their time quarrelling.

Sita raised her dark eyes from the notepaper to the window. After staring at the darkness outside for a while, she turned her eyes back inside the room. To the wall and the clock. To Saroj's portrait. And instantly that face, that horrifying face, floated up before her eyes.

She shut the drawer quickly, trying to turn her eyes away from Saroj's portrait. But she could not. A face, a terrifying face, attracted her like a lingering kiss.

The very next moment Saroj, who was in his study, heard her scream, a scream that had become all too familiar by now: There! There!

Saroj ran into the room. Into the second-floor room. Sita was unconscious again. She had slumped on to the floor.

Dr Roy was due at seven in the evening. He was never unpunctual, not even by a minute. He was very strict. He would talk to the patient alone, without anyone else present. He had already informed everyone that this was how mental illnesses were treated.

Saroj was sitting by Sita's bed. Although she had regained consciousness, she lay with her eyes closed. It was a quarter to seven. A servant arrived to inform Saroj of a telephone call. He left on tiptoe.

Sita turned on her side. She felt a discomfort inside her head. Not exactly a pain, but much worse. There was no one in the room, she observed. Saroj must have gone out for something. The rajanigandha on the table was beginning to spread its fragrance now. A gust of wind came in through the gap in the curtain to distribute the scent all over the room. The wall clock showed thirteen minutes to seven. Sita was having trouble breathing. She dabbed her handkerchief on her perspiring forehead. The handkerchief was cool with the aroma of lavender. Saroj had switched the light off, as Sita had asked. The light hurt her eyes. A faint light in the veranda was visible through the curtains. Everything in the room was indistinct in the darkness at dusk.

With a deep sigh, Sita turned on her side again. In the darkness, someone came up near her head on light footsteps. Who is it, Sita asked, her eyes still closed.

No movements now, came a gentle reply. Stay as you are. Tell me everything about your illness, all right? Don't leave anything out.

Oh, it's Dr Roy. Take a seat, please.

Please don't worry about me, stay as you are, don't open your eyes.

Sita was feeling a great discomfort inside her head. She couldn't bear it any more.

Very well, I'll tell you everything. Listen. This has been going on for four or five months. I was on my way back from a music session at Gitabitan one evening, it was around 8 p.m. My car stopped at a traffic signal at the crossing of Circular Road and Chowringhee. Suddenly I saw a man under a lamp post, glaring at me. It felt awful, terrible. He was tall, thin. One of his eyes seemed to be popping out. His hair was dishevelled, he had a stubble on his cheeks. His jaw was slack, as though it belonged to someone else. His mouth had fallen open, the tongue hanging out slightly.

You obviously observed him quite closely.

Yes. Sita continued listlessly: Besides, it's not as though I saw him just once, I've seen him many times since then. I felt so scared. He smiled at me, displaying his ugly, crooked teeth. A dirty, frayed suit hung loosely on him. My skin prickled with fear. I told the driver to drive away quickly. But that repulsive and frightening face took over my consciousness, in sleep and in wakefulness. I had never seen him before, and yet I couldn't help feeling all the time that I knew him. Such a horrible, pale, clammy face.

And then?

Sita paused for breath. There were beads of perspiration on her forehead. Her veins had become visible next to her closed eyes—blue veins. Tucking one of her hands under her pillow, Sita continued: Whenever I went out after that,

I felt the man would be waiting for me somewhere. About to get into my car after shopping at New Market, I might find him standing at the gate, squinting at me, or staring without blinking. I would close the car door quickly. Ever since then, I have been consumed by a terrible fear. I saw him several times at different places on the road. I'll tell you one particular incident. I was visiting a friend at her place. She dropped me close to my home late in the evening. The rest of the way was quite desolate. Only the occasional lamp post lit up the road. Suddenly I wondered what would happen if I were to run into that man. I began to tremble with fear. Looking behind me, I saw him hobbling towards me, about five or six yards away. My limbs froze. I practically ran home. I could hear someone limping behind me, continuously. Entering through the gate, I ran into the hall and fainted.

Sita paused. Her face had turned ashen with agitation and fear. There wasn't a sound in the room. Saroj could be heard talking at the bottom of the stairs. He was on the phone. The curtain swayed slightly in the breeze. The air was heavy with the scent of flowers.

For a long time, continued Sita, I didn't tell my husband. He was busy with different things, so was I. But one day I did tell him. He laughed it off. Are you turning prematurely senile? he asked. Have you started daydreaming? The durwan hasn't seen anyone like this man near the gate. You'd better rest for a few days. But, Dr Roy, that was when my illness took hold of me.

Continue, please, came the unhurried response.

Then there was an accident one day. A small girl had been run over. The mob was busy beating the driver up. I spotted the man in the crowd. He was staring greedily at the blood-soaked body of the little girl—an obscene delight written all over his face. My driver took the little girl into the car to take her to the hospital. I saw the man wagging his finger in the crowd, threatening me. I can't tell you what an awful nightmare I had that night, Dr Roy. I dreamt I was lying on the operation table in a hospital. Someone appeared near my head to anaesthetize me—it was the same man. I screamed and fainted. The illness has become much worse since then. I live in fear of seeing that face all the time. I cannot sleep at night. My heart's extremely weak. I can't take it any more. Dr Roy—Sita spoke loudly in her agitation—either you must cure me quickly, or I must die. I can't go on like this.

With a deep sigh, Sita remained in bed, her eyes closed. Her beautiful, fair brow was covered in perspiration, her exhausted face looked heartbroken. The room was dark. Almost nothing was visible. Only a faint beam of light entered the room through the gap between the curtains.

You've never seen that man at home, have you?

No, I'd have died on the spot.

Is he very ugly?

Very. I have no words for it.

Something like this?

A face leant over the bed. Opening her eyes, Sita screamed.

No one who'd heard that terrified scream would ever forget it.

Sita! Sita! Putting the phone down, Saroj hobbled upstairs.

Sita's body lay inert on the bed. There was no one in the room.

Saroj laid his ear to her breast to check for a heartbeat. When he realized that this heart would never beat again, his protruding eyes suddenly acquired a strange look.

As soon as the clock rang seven in the hall, Dr Bikash Roy's car was heard sounding its horn.

Translated from the original
Bengali 'Mukh' by Arunava Sinha

BIRTH NIGHT

Kiran Manral

Kiran Manral's books include *The Face at the Window, The Reluctant Detective, Once upon a Crush, All Aboard, Karmic Kids: The Story of Parenting Nobody Told You, A Boy's Guide to Growing Up* and *Saving Maya.* Her short-story collections include *Switcheroo* and *True Love Stories.*

It was cold. So very cold and dark. She was trapped in an inky black darkness. Was it a dream, a nightmare? Had she moved into another dimension where nothing was as it seemed and everything was cold, stony, unfamiliar, the stench of decay in the air, the sense of things crawling around her, within her, unsettling her? And then it hit her. She was trapped beneath the earth, flung into a hastily dug grave. And nestled next to her was a tiny, rigid, cold body that should have been suckling at her breast.

She woke up with a start. It was a low moon, hanging at the edge of the sky as though placed there as an afterthought, a moon that would rather be somewhere else. The room was bathed in moonlight, cold, silvery, mercurial, as it crept in insidiously, inching over the floorboards, and from there on to the legs of the bed, stealing slowly over the covers of the bed, and then on to her, as she sat up abruptly, chilled to the bone. The nights were dark in these hills, dark and silent. And cold. So very cold. Like her dream.

Sometime in the course of the night the half-hearted fire in the fireplace had gone out. The smell of burnt wood hung in the icy room. A few days more. Just a few days more, she told herself. The baby in her stomach had settled down now, awaiting its birth. The kicking had long stopped, there was no space in the tight confines of the womb to kick any more; a sudden bump, a stretching of the skin already taut with the forced expansion to contain it, was a stab of pain each time. She sat back against the headboard, feeling the constant unease of pregnancy acutely. Sleeping comfortably was impossible now, the weight of the baby made it difficult to turn easily, her legs locked themselves into painful cramps. The pressed-upon bladder, which demanded emptying every couple of hours. And then there were the dreams, the terrible dreams.

They had begun a month or so ago, dreams that took over and dragged her off into a realm where it was forever night, dark and menacing. The bed was cold and hard, like an ice block. She was thirsty in the strange way one is always thirsty when one wakes from deep sleep and a discomfiting dream, when no amount of water sates one's thirst, except when the thirst itself decides it has been slaked. She poured herself a glass of water from the jug on the bedside table. It felt heavy; she barely had any strength left within her to function with a degree of normalcy. The baby growing inside her was steadily leaching out all the strength from her. It was a parasite, that's what it was, this child. A parasite. It had not only sucked away all the joy from her life, and had her flung into this far-fetched corner of the world in a remote hill-station, but had drained away everything that made her proud of herself—her beauty, her light-footedness, her blooming complexion. She was now, as she looked at herself in the mirror opposite the bed, silvery white from the moonlight falling full on her, ghoulish.

The glass fell from her hand. The face looking back at her from the mirror was hers and yet not hers. She fell back against the pillows, drawing the rough blankets up to her face, peering at the woman she saw opposite. It was her. She must have been hallucinating. Or was it a trick of the light? She was dishevelled, there were dark shadows under her eyes, her face had become gaunt and hollow. These last months of pregnancy had not been kind to her. And then, the incessant rain had compelled her to stay indoors all the time, making her even sallower than she had been to begin with. *Gori mem.* White-skinned. That was what had attracted him to her, the white skin. He would place his hand, brown and swarthy, on her belly and marvel at the contrast in skin tones, before gently sliding his fingers into the place no one before him had ever touched. She had been helpless to resist him; he had both charm and a dangerous edge that made him irresistible. And there was the aura of command that came to him by birth. How could she have resisted being seduced?

She put a hand to her swollen belly, feeling it tentatively. She could feel the bumps and hard angles where the baby pushed against the skin, trying to find more space to manoeuvre itself into comfort. Some nights she dreamt that the baby had torn her stomach open and emerged, covered with blood. On others, she felt a strange overwhelming sense of being one with the foetus, the distinct sensation that she was not alone in her body. If she closed her eyes, she could hear the baby talking to her in a language that was not made up of distinct words but one she could understand clearly. 'Mother,' the baby said, 'save me.' She had no reply. 'Mother!' it would come again, more insistent, a persistent repetition that pounded at the base of her cranium, resounded within the folds of her skull, swirling in continuous loops through the flabby folds of the brain that kept her functional. 'Mother, save me.'

She felt a tear trickle down the side of her cheek, and drop on to the cold bedspread. The woman in the mirror looking back at her was her. The woman in the mirror was not her.

She struck a match and lit the candle in the stand next to the bedside. It flickered uncertainly for the briefest moment before flaring into a determined flame that swayed enticingly with each slight draught that came through the cracks between the windowsill and the pane.

'Anytime now,' the good doctor had told her when he'd last come to visit her a couple of days ago on his weekly rounds. He would cycle up from his clinic down in town, a spry fifty-year-old, kept fit by the need to cycle up steep hill roads to visit patients. 'Be ready.' He was kindly, this doctor, he brought her books to read so that she could while away the interminable days as she waited for the baby to be born. He did not ask the uncomfortable questions about why she was kept in isolation for the entire duration of her confinement, and why she had been forbidden from interacting with anyone in the area. '*Angrezi mem,*' the children who ran across the long paths beyond the garden of the cottage called her. They had no reticence about peeking into windows and picking up the one-sided conversations the pretty woman had with the baby in her stomach. She stopped sitting down in the long veranda that ran around the house when it became difficult for her to walk, when her face became gaunt and haunted, and her growing belly robbed all the flesh off her bones into its giant protuberance.

A sudden spear of lightning slashed the sky into unequal halves. The sound of raindrops falling heavily on the roof interrupted the hushed quietude. A storm was not expected.

It frightened her. Her heartbeat began accelerating violently in her bony chest cavity. The low, displeased growl of thunder followed almost immediately, shaking the roof of the cottage, rattling the windows in their frames. A sudden sharp piercing of pain slit through her belly, and she felt the first acute spasm, which knocked her breathless. A sudden gush from between her thighs and her water broke all over the bed, making it a cold, damp swamp with no refuge. She fumbled for the little bell by the side of her bed and rang it with trembling fingers. The sound echoed in the hushed silence that waited predatorily before the storm broke out. Footsteps clamoured across the wooden boarding and the door was pushed open urgently. A huge man stood in the doorway, his face crumpled with sleep and disapproval.

'*Kya hua*, memsahib?' he asked, his burly arms holding on to the jamb of the door, more a prison than the closed door could ever hope to be.

'Call the doctor,' she said, throwing out the words with great difficulty as a contraction grabbed her again and tossed her on the high waves of pain, crests she rode and dismounted as the world turned to a blur of red and purple beyond her closed eyelids.

He shut the door behind him, his footsteps hurrying as they echoed down the stairs and then faded away. She could hear calls and raised voices from the servant quarters. Slower, gentler footsteps made their way now to the door; a wizened old woman peered in. 'It has begun,' she said, in the native dialect, and then yelled instructions at other unknown persons to get hot water and towels, and to boil a sharp knife.

She then entered the room, and put her hands on the swollen belly, feeling it with her eyes closed. Picking up the lit, flickering candle, she peered up into the wet nether regions, which were stretching apart excruciatingly.

'The baby is upside down. I think I can see the feet. I hope that rascal goes quickly to get the doctor sahib. Wait, what is this . . . ?' She looked perplexed, and then helped her off the bed and got the wet bedding off, turning the mattress over with an almost superhuman strength, given the slightness of her frame. 'Here, lie down now.'

And so she did, tossing and turning through what seemed like an eternity of contractions that came in waves and threatened to tear her apart, until she finally drifted into a dim, grey fog where voices came to her from a distance, and hands worked on her body and she was there and not there. There was a sense of something slipping through her and emerging and a collective gasp from the people standing in the room, and then a wet slick gush of something else slipping through her again. She heard the doctor's voice, urgent and demanding, as he asked for something in the native dialect. Voices swirled in hushed tones around her. Someone, she didn't know who, had brought in a lamp at some point and the shadows thrown on the walls moved independently of those who made them.

'She's losing too much blood, she might not survive,' said the doctor.

'It's all right,' replied the burly man. 'She's not required now. And since that the child is a girl, it is not required too.' She felt the world going black around her as she sank into a dead faint.

She was walking through a garden dappled with the rays of morning sunlight. The fresh scent of newly cut grass punctuated the air, interspersed with the soft fragrance of the rose bushes that edged it. The green of the grass and the blue of the sky so bright it hurt her eyes. She knew the sun was shining but the rays did not give any warmth. Holding her hand was a young girl, with eyes as blue as aquamarines. 'Mother, don't leave me,' the child said. A cool breeze flew in at that moment, chilling her to the bone, blotting out the sun with gigantic black clouds. The earth split open with a resounding crack and she fell into it. The child, her hands reaching out from the edge of the chasm, receded into a small dot in the distance as she fell farther and farther into an abyss that had no end. And then she opened her eyes.

In the crib next to the bed, swaddled in a white cloth, was an infant, eyes closed in deep sleep. She looked around. It was morning, the sun was bright in the east, pale yellow rays stretching out across the pink-tipped peaks in the distance, slowly staking their claim over the rest of the world. The birds were all atwitter in the trees fringing the tiny garden that marked the periphery of the cottage. She picked up the bell and rang it, struggling to get to her feet, feeling the gushing of the blood between her thighs. She could barely stand. The door opened and the old lady from the previous evening came in, holding her with a cool hand while she hobbled out to the bathroom, the blood dripping from between her thighs to the wooden floor—both an indictment and a curse.

'Is the baby okay?' she asked the woman. 'Eyes, ears, fingers, toes, everything?'

The woman nodded. 'The baby is fine, but she was born veiled. Her feet down. This child will have the gift.'

She held the wall, shakily. 'What gift?'

'When she grows you will know.'

She put it out of her head and went into the bathroom, the stitches stinging as she urinated. Her belly, now deflated and loose, flapped in front of her like an excess pouch of skin. She looked at herself in the cracking silvering of the mirror above the washbasin, and stepped back in horror.

The voice in her head had stopped. She could hear herself think again. She was alone in her body once again. But then, it came back. 'Mother,' the voice spoke to her again, floating out of the ether. 'Mother, don't abandon me,' it said. 'Come to me.' This time it spoke from around her, not from within her. She sank heavily into the corner of the bathtub, holding the basin for support. It was the weakness that was making her hallucinate this way. There was no other explanation. Her baby was sleeping in her crib, peacefully.

She splashed water on her face. It was icy and startled her into complete wakefulness. Surely she was imagining the voice in her head. Surely, the child outside in the crib wasn't able to project her thoughts into her head. There was a sharp knock at the door of the bathroom.

'Are you all right?' asked the woman who was in charge of her welfare. 'If you want to bathe, let me know, I will heat up the water for you.'

'No, I don't want to bathe, I'm coming out.'

She stuffed some rolls of cloth between her legs to staunch the incessant flow of blood that seemed to be waterfalling out of her. The woman was standing on the landing, staring with a strange expression on her face as she saw her struggle to walk towards the bedroom, her knees almost collapsing from weakness.

Her chest was getting turgid, a swelling that demanded the release of a child suckling on it. 'I need to nurse my baby,' she said, moving towards the crib. There was nothing there, it was empty. 'They just took her away,' the woman said, with that strange expression which was a mix of pity and empathy. 'Her father's people, they came and took her away while you were in the bathroom.'

She screamed, a visceral scream that echoed through the boards and planks of the cottage, it hollowed her out. 'No, no . . .' and began staggering down the stairs, reaching the front door with great effort, wrenching it open just as a car roared off into the distance, the smoke it released merging with the slight fog that the September day had brought with it. 'My baby, my baby . . .' she sobbed, collapsing to her knees at the doorway, uncaring that the air was chill and she was clad only in a thin nightdress.

The old woman had followed her to the door. She helped her back to her feet and led her up to the bedroom. 'You did know, didn't you, that he would take the child away? I've been instructed to tell you that you are free to go wherever you want now, when you're feeling well enough to travel. Your tickets will be booked for you.'

She had nowhere to go. No family to go back to. No job to go back to; her position as governess to the daughters of the royal family had effectively ended when she got herself pregnant by their father. She lay back on the bed and wondered what would have happened had she had a boy. He would have adopted the boy legally and made the illegitimate child his legal heir. She would have been set up for life in a corner of the country, on the condition that she never spoke about her relationship with him, like he had promised. But she had given birth to a daughter. A daughter was of no use to him, he already had three of his own between his two wives. She lay on the bed, feeling the blood leak out of her body and the unsuckled milk harden into painful lumps in her chest.

The day segued into night. She remained immobile on the bed, her mind a grey blankness. The old woman came up with a plate of food. Rice, a thin gruel of lentils lightly tempered with spices. 'Eat,' she commanded. 'You need your strength for the journey. Have you thought about where you want to go?'

She shook her head to reply in the negative. The tone of the voice speaking to her changed, there was a gentleness to it now, an unexpected tenderness that made her eyes sting with unshed tears.

'These men can be such bastards,' the old woman said, not expecting a reply. She didn't get any.

The plate with the food was still wafting thin tendrils of smoke. She sat up gingerly and took the plate from the side table it was kept on and tried to get some morsels of food past the coagulated lump that had formed in her throat. She handed the plate back. 'I can't eat.' The woman took it and went out, her footsteps now soundless on the wooden planks. She stood up and moved to the window.

The September night was blotted with clouds, a restless moon shone unevenly on to the ground, its light filtered through wisps of clouds. The patch of garden leading to the main road was filled with shadows, each blade of grass reflecting the silvery moonlight like so many individual spears poised to break through the calm of the night.

'Mother,' said a voice again. 'Don't leave me alone.' She heard it with her ears this time. A voice that was not a voice, but silvery and spectral. She started with shock and looked around the room. She was hallucinating. That was the only thing that could explain this. She was going mad. She put her hands over her ears and closed her eyes. 'Mother, mother,' the voice spoke again, a thin voice that was a child's yet not a child's.

She opened her eyes again. Strangely they were drawn to a corner of the garden where there was a patch of ground that had no grass, just a mound of freshly dug mud heaped up in a small pile; it looked, she realized with a sudden stab to her heart, just the right size for a grave. A small grave, enough to bury a newborn. She pulled on her wrap, which had been on the chair, discarded from the previous night when she'd still had her child within her and the reflection in the mirror had not been hers. She ran out of her room, opened the front door and rushed to the little corner bereft of grass or the dignity of a gravestone. The old woman came hurtling out behind her, picking her up from where she lay sobbing on the ground. 'It was born dead, there was nothing we could do . . . It was a boy. Yes, you had twins, my child, the boy was born dead, the girl survived.'

Sobs tore through her, lacerating her body. She sobbed for the child she had lost to death and the one she had lost to destiny. The woman helped her back to her room and tucked her in, rubbing her hands and feet to warm her up. She bustled around, stepping out and getting fresh kindling for the fireplace, and lighting it up, before coercing her to gulp from a medicinal bottle of brandy, and forcing a hot-water bottle into the covers against her body.

'Ring the bell if you feel unwell,' she said, as she closed the door behind her. 'Going out in these thin clothes, when she's just delivered, what was she thinking?' she grumbled to no one in particular. There was silence except for the crackle from the fireplace and the hissing of the sparks as they shot up the chimney.

'Mother,' the voice came again. She sat up with a start. 'Mother, don't leave me alone in the ground. It's cold here.'

The mirror opposite, lit by the moonlight streaming now into the room, reflected her. She looked terrible. It was the blood loss, she told herself, it was making her hear things. And then the woman in the mirror smiled at her, holding up a gurgling baby who turned his head and looked at her. 'Mother,' the voice of the baby rang in her ears. 'Come to me.'

When the old woman came into the room in the morning with the tray bearing the pot of tea and biscuits, she stepped on the thin stream of congealed blood that had flowed from the slit wrists all night. She screamed aloud and dropped the tray, running to get people for help, someone from the neighbouring cottage.

The body on the bed lay unmoving, the life force extinguished. In the mirror opposite, she was sitting up, examining the slits on her wrists and looking on, waiting, a wait that would last for years until the bed was occupied again, with the promise of more blood to be shed.

GHOST NO. 1

Shinie Antony

Shinie Antony has authored the short-story collections *The Orphanage for Words, Barefoot and Pregnant* and the novel *When Mira Went Forth and Multiplied,* She has compiled the anthology *Why We Don't Talk.* She won the Commonwealth Short Story Prize for the Asia region in 2003. *The Girl Who Couldn't Love* is her latest novel.

Once upon a time there was no time, no 'once'. Only he and I. A good man, a bad woman. There we were, naked and curious, dying to know, just know. But soon it all changed, and shame and lust, hot and thick, covered us in fumes. Before that of course there was that incident with the snake. And a fruit . . . An apple, I think.

We got new lodgings. Much sex followed, many kids. I was revered and reviled. Here and there I have come across altars dedicated to me. I am, as they say, the first woman. Fresh off the boat XX chromosomes. I am Eve. Before corsets and foundation creams. Before red-light areas and refrigerators. It had been so lonely, not knowing about gender discrimination or domestic labour or glass ceilings or marital rape or household appliances. Yeah, yeah, daughters came and grand-daughters who then became my daughters-in-law and grand-daughters-in-law, since there was no other family around to marry into. But they were too young, they were little girls, babies. I didn't sit around and gossip with them.

And Adam? Too busy inventing and discovering, making fire and tracking water. A workaholic who left first thing in the morning and went on business trips barefoot all over earth. We barely spoke—language itself was still under construction—and what we did fast and furious late into

197

night required little speech. No TV, no Wi-Fi; we get bored, I miss a period.

Time went by and one evening (or perhaps it looked like evening because my sight was mostly gone, there were no glasses yet and I could see not much) I stopped moving, stopped breathing. But since I was the first to die no one had any idea of my passing and my body lay in that position till it fell apart into dust from time and disuse.

I swapped dimensions and became that thing called a ghost. Officially, the world's very first ghost. Pets had died before me but they were all animal-shaped spirits, on their fours, circling hedges, wagging tails; fish ghosts swam transparently in seas and ghost turtles raced ghost hares. I was not only the first human ghost, but also the first female ghost. My breasts smoke rings, uterus water vapour. And residual kitchen steam that hung like a halo around what used to be my head. Hair tied that tight for a lifetime leaves the scalp tingling long into the afterworld.

At first I roamed around aimlessly, the equivalent of my future mall-wanderer counterpart, going from bark to ballgown to bikini in spectre couture. I skimmed pebbles and blew bubbles in ponds. And then I began to hear the voices around me. 'Oh,' I thought (for I had no idea until then), 'I am a ghost.' No one could see me, I could see everyone. With no idea or example of what ghosts did, I began to stalk women. You see that frail-looking one crossing over into the forest to relieve herself? I stood guard and escorted her back, only to watch in horror as her man savaged her with a log. She made no protest, expressed no doubt, instead she apologized, she obeyed, she did as she was bidden. She was me as I used to be, I realized. I was invisible but it was like looking into a mirror.

I spent my time trailing after the women as they went about giving birth, rearing kids and cooking and cleaning and generally being so boring I felt I was dying all over again. Timelines began to blur and that is when I started to think backwards, to flashback to that time when I . . . did not do as told. They did make a hue and cry about that, but just for a moment let's dwell on the delicious rise of brows, hands on hips, mouth open in the 'o' of no.

I shook my head, sighed and rolled my eyes at the women. 'Talk back,' I'd try to scream, spraying mist from my imaginary throat.

And then it happened. I was floating an inch above the ground in a cave when this man came in after having lain with his neighbour's woman—and I say 'lain' just because I am a literal sort, concussed as she was by a precoital blow to the head. Where was I? Yes, yes, levitating, minding my own business when he began to beat his wife up. First he wakes her from a deep exhausted sleep and then he bashes her. *With her own baby.*

I was standing right behind her, closer than her shadow, breathing out as she breathed in, when whoosh I was inside her—I *was* her. When I lifted my hand, up came hers. And she . . . I . . . we . . . slapped and slapped him. Weakened by his previous bout of rough sex he was no match for the two of us and soon fell over with a most surprised look on his face. We ran out then to dance in the rain. When I left her she was still dancing.

This was such fun. I began to travel. Soon another ghost popped up, and another, the same gender as me, so that together we set about being, I guess, super-ghosts. We coined a short signature tune that we hummed as we zoomed about the planet, swishing and swashing on our way to rescuing women, our pretend backsides twitching like bloodhound noses. Giving them the words. The questions. The doubts. The facts.

I just slip in and out of them, no one sees. Meek, gentle women, with years of nodding behind them, were being possessed routinely. The name-calling was plain-salted: witch/bitch, menopaused and 'Is she a man?'.

Come on.

They see only the asking woman, her with the why and the what and the how. They don't see me, the first woman, carefully fitting my soul into hers, my gums to her gums, focusing with all might on being a mouth.

On moonless nights I paste words, delicately and lovingly, on girl tongues. Words that fight, shake a fist, or whisper softly to win. Soon phantom females were everywhere, the dead doing their bit for the dying, for the barely living. Male ghosts disappeared monosyllabically into caves never to be seen again; after a lifetime of performance anxiety they wanted to put away their thing forever. I, on the other hand, expanded my vocabulary. Learnt to say no in all languages.

But enough about me. Ghosts have work to do. Yes, you, open your gob. Let me coat your sweet little tongue with dissent. This will hurt a little. Focus, my beautiful descendant. We have a no to say.

THE HOWLING

Jaishree Misra

Jaishree Misra has written eight novels and also edited an anthology of writings on motherhood, published by Zubaan and Save the Children India. She has an MA in English literature from Kerala University and two postgraduate diplomas from the University of London, in Special Education and Broadcast Journalism. A non-fiction book on Kerala will be published in 2017.

Midnight and it had started again, the howling. I'd heard it every night for the past three. Ever since I arrived in the border town of Bikaner, the third stop on my India travels. It began low, almost a murmur, and gradually built up into a mournful wail before becoming this huge, full-blooded howl.

It was almost funny, the way all the horror clichés were being ticked off (stroke of midnight, unexplained howling, the still quiet of desert nights, locals pretending like they knew nothing). Well, I would have found it funny had I not been so terrified. At six foot plus, and blessed with my father's butch physique, I was not normally scared of much but this, this maniacal howling had for three nights now grabbed at my very intestines and turned them inside out. I'd never known anything like it before.

I lay in my bed, listening once again to the unearthly ululation, the hair on my arms and legs prickling and rising, my heart racing as though I were running a marathon. For the hundredth time I tried to convince myself that the origin of the howling was canine. But to cling to that hope was fooling myself. I worked as a police dog trainer back in London and knew those creatures intimately. In fact, I'd had dogs since I was a child and was well familiar with all the sounds they were capable of producing. There were some members of my doggy family who were eerily human in interaction and communication but even they could not have produced a howl like this.

No, this sound undeniably derived from a person, man or woman, and was full of the kind of pain and betrayal only a fellow human would accuse anyone of. In all my years of dog rearing, I knew the canine species—even the fiercest of them— as stupidly friendly and forgiving creatures, incapable of the kind of contempt this howl contained. This was no normal scream of pain or frustration or anger even. Instead, it spoke strangely of yearnings and some kind of deep, unforgiven treachery. It was definitely, definitely human.

Just as on the previous two nights, it went on renting the night air for precisely five minutes (a longer five-minute spell there has never been) and then, just as abruptly as it had started, it stopped. I lay frozen, expecting it to begin again. The pain was clearly not fully expressed yet. The silence that followed was pregnant with unspoken anguish. Surely there would be another scream. Another searing howl. But no. Nothing but the silence of the night. And the echoing of that primal sound in my ears, in the very chambers of my heart.

Of course, I could not sleep for long afterwards. Just as on the previous two nights. Tossing and turning on the bed of the tourist lodge I'd carefully chosen on Trip Advisor, I resolved to move on the next day. Go back to Jodhpur perhaps, or Jaisalmer. Anywhere but this desert town with its nocturnal banshees.

Anyway, I'd seen the fort of golden sandstone the town was famous for, wandered around in the watery winter sunshine, taken some moody black-and-white shots of archways and ramparts despite the throbbing headache, brought on no doubt by my two sleepless nights. I'd peered into the small doorway set within the main door of the fort with some trepidation, convinced that the howling had emanated from its cavernous interiors. On entering the first of the rooms, my heart lurched wildly for a split second when a small grey figure leapt out of a narrow window but it turned out to be a fucking monkey, a mangy creature with a grinning face and a red arse.

Everything else looked benign in the daytime. Except for the faint smell of bat shit in a few of the rooms, there was nothing to indicate the presence of spooks or haunts of any sort.

Tonight was also condemned to sleeplessness, I realized, as I pulled again at the spare blanket I'd asked for, hoping being warmer would aid better sleep. But that infernal, ghastly howling just would not leave my head.

The next morning, after what must have been a fitful bout of dawn sleep, I stumbled out of my room in search of the manager of the lodge.

He was already at his desk, luckily, and I tackled him without any of the usual pleasantries. I saw no reason to indulge the man, given how torrid a time I was having in his guest house.

'Mr Chauhan, I'd like to cut short my stay here, please.'

His tone was annoyingly solicitous and concerned. 'Why, sir, why? Hope there is not any problem?'

'It's a real problem, actually, Mr Chauhan. Though I don't suppose it's your fault.'

'What is it, please tell me? Maybe I can fix it, even if it is not our fault.'

I laughed. 'Well, you'd have to acknowledge there is a problem first. Yesterday, I could not even get anyone here to admit there was anything wrong at all so how can I hope for understanding?'

'What is wrong, sir? Please tell me.'

'Well, it's that bloody howling again. In the middle of the night. That only I'm able to hear, apparently.'

'Again? You heard it again?'

I nodded and watched him ring the buzzer next to his desk. He maintained the look of concern although the expression on his face was still disbelieving. 'Yesterday, my boys were saying they heard nothing at all, sir. And two of them live on the premises so, if this howling was as loud as you say, they should have heard it too.'

I sucked in my breath but by now one of the guards had appeared in the doorway. The manager turned to him. 'Pradeep, Mr Smeaton here says that he heard that howling sound again last night.'

The guard produced his best blank look. 'When, sir?'

'Last night,' I snapped. 'Midnight. Just as before. Three fucking nights now. Three!'

The guard and manager went into a flurry of Hindi before the latter turned back to me.

'He is saying that it is just not possible, sir.'

'I can assure you I'm not making it up. I have heard this howling for three days now. It starts at midnight, lasts five minutes or thereabouts and then stops. So not that long. But it's so bloody loud and piercing that anyone in this guest house will hear it. Even if they're drunk or fast asleep. Unless you're suggesting that I'm the only person hearing it and am crazy or something.'

'No, no, sir. Will I ever say that? Never, never. But it is not just the guards, sir. I believe none of the other guests are also complaining.'

I got up, my chair screeching. 'Well, I'm hardly likely to go around checking with every other guest, am I? So, if this is all a ruse to prevent me from getting my money back, I don't really care any more. I just want to get the hell out of here.'

Having delivered that final shot, I left. Returning to my room, I started to throw my clothes into my backpack and, within fifteen minutes, I was walking out of the lodge in the direction of the bus stand. In the distance, the fort glowed golden in the sun and, despite the beauty of its silhouette, I shivered at whatever malevolent spirit wandered its corridors every night.

———

It was afternoon by the time my bus crawled into Jaisalmer. The road had been bumpy and my body felt as though my skeleton was rattling around loose inside it. I dragged myself down the main strip in town, eyeing the different B&Bs and trying to figure out one that would be both cheap and comfortable.

Finally choosing the Raj Inn, I stretched out on my bed, feeling its unfamiliar hardness beneath me, testing to see if it would give me that one good night's sleep that had eluded me these past few days.

I pulled my phone out of the pocket of my jacket and turned on the mobile data I was conserving so carefully. I had no idea how much this sort of thing cost in India but something told me it wouldn't be cheap. A scattering of emails and WhatsApps fell across the screen like black snow. 'Simon', 'Mother', 'British Gas', 'Transport for London' . . . May as well go chronologically, I thought, clicking open Simon's email from a couple of days ago.

Hey mate. Sorry to bring bad news when you're on holiday but I thought you needed to know that Alicia's done something drastic. She was pretty devastated after you broke up with her and left for India. And, in the light of her MS diagnosis I suppose I should have sympathy. Mustn't beat about the bush so I'll just say it as it is. Don't know whether it was just a cry for attention but, last Sat night, she went and slashed her wrists (yes, both of them). Her neighbour found her bleeding and unconscious on her sofa, rushed her to hospital etc., etc., but it was too late, mate. Alicia's dead. No other way to put it. She's gone, mate, and I thought I'd better let you know sooner rather than later. Spoke to your mother but she too didn't know the Indian number to get you on as your UK one was switched off. Resorting to email as you'll probably check these off and on. Where are you now? Don't suppose I can wish you good travels in the light of this but I didn't want you to be the last one to find out in case you wanted to make some contact with her parents. Sorry again to be the bearer of such horrible news. Call me when you can. Take care. Si.

I looked out of the window. It wasn't dark yet. But I knew it would not be long before the howling started again.